Who will marry me?

Edward Mutema

WESTBOW
PRESS®
A DIVISION OF THOMAS NELSON
& ZONDERVAN

WestBow Press books may be ordered through booksellers or by contacting:

WestBow Press
A Division of Thomas Nelson & Zondervan
1663 Liberty Drive
Bloomington, IN 47403
www.westbowpress.com
844-714-3454

ISBN: 978-1-6642-5826-6 (sc)
ISBN: 978-1-6642-5827-3 (hc)
ISBN: 978-1-6642-5828-0 (e)

Library of Congress Control Number: 2022903186

Print information available on the last page.

WestBow Press rev. date: 04/12/2022

Contents

Chapter 1

There was an eerie silence. The wall clock ticked loudly, muffling the sound of the blurting heartbeats of Mum and Dad. This was odd. No daughter or son of the family had aggressively asked this question before. It was taboo in the village. Boys and girls had been whipped for such misplaced courage. But this was no village, or town, or Africa. The village was six thousand miles away. There were no elders to talk to, no aunties and uncles to consult.

Reality set in. The very daughter they thought would timidly stroll through life unquestioningly had suddenly gathered some hyena courage. Life had become so visible and stark that she demanded an answer before it was too late. She was on the verge of plunging into the unknown unless someone led her along the narrow and truthful path. It was now or never. She waited with bated breath. The last drop of saliva trickled down her dry throat, almost choking her. She swallowed her breath and suspended her heartbeat for as long as she could.

Suddenly the phone rang. Not once, not twice, but repeatedly. No one seemed to have the courage to answer it.

It was a welcome intruder in a room where even silence had died. "Why are you sitting there as if you can't hear the phone ringing?" Dad spoke rather gently in a husky voice trapped by the intermittent gasping for breath resulting from his daughter's question.

She sprang up from the bean bag where she had slipped uncomfortably as she had waited for an answer. Melissa carefully held the phone to her ear and politely said. "I am sorry; Dad is busy. Can you try later?" then she hung up. She threw herself on the bean bag. Her face said it all. A sense of guilt perhaps. She had lied about her dad. She had to put pressure on her mum and dad to say something.

And as she sat upright, staring at her mother, she carried on from where she had left off. Looking at her mum she cautiously carried on from where she had left, "So, who will marry me, Mum and Dad, in a country where there are fewer boys of my tribe and more of the other? You have always taught us to pray and to go to church, but there are no men to marry in church either. I am serious, Mum." Both Mum and Dad looked aghast at the courage of their last child.

Mum thought, *Why is she insisting on an answer now? What is prompting her? This is weird. She knows that if she prays, she will get a good man to marry her.* But Mum could not verbalize her thoughts. She had seen many young boys and girls living with their partners, under pressure to cohabit because similar questions had not been addressed. She knew families who were heartbroken and had lost control of their children because they were afraid to tackle these life-threatening issues. Many were incapable of doing so because they themselves had faltered on the road to lifelong marriage. They had messed up when they were in the village. They did not know what to do in these circumstances. Their experiences did not match what their children were demanding answers for.

Conversations in the village were not so abrupt. They were always taken to their logical conclusion. Not this time. Melissa's dad Takura, or TK, was the typical village boy. He had been brought up to revere his culture. He knew the ins and outs of their tribe's behaviour. What was expected of him as a boy included a mixture of male chauvinism and a tint of identity preservation. The night vigils were a breeding ground for real men and women, who lived by the book and dared not mess with what their parents taught them. Soon after their initiation, the girls in the village would be clad with red bands signifying their readiness for true love and marriage. Boys looked for such when they contemplated marriage. The girls were protected by their aunts, who literally escorted them wherever they went to protect them from the male vultures, who too were on the boil seeking whom they may devour! Such was the systemic cultural organization. You hardly found boys and girls eloping. It was a given that a conducive marriage environment was created that would enable would-be candidates to easily pick and choose the girls of their choice. That was the way TK's parents had done it, and he also expected his children to follow suit.

But then war broke out. Families were scattered. Young men and women left in droves to join the guerrilla army. Girls became soldiers overnight. What was taboo yesterday became the new normal. Traditions remained intact but under pressure from the demands of combat. The war period upset what was deemed to be the identity of a people. Preservation became a challenge and, when the war ended, many left for other untested shores. With the economic downturn, scores of young families and older ones sought greener pastures in what became the diaspora. This was a place in limbo, where culture had no fixed abode. Many were determined to reap their harvest and quickly return home. It soon became a pipe dream years after the target date had expired. There was no other home. This was home. Period.

TK was not the only one in this predicament. Many of his age were also caught up in this. His girls were extremely intelligent. One a lawyer, another just graduated from medical school, and the last one a senior carer in a nursing home. All at a ripe old age. If they had been "home," they would either been married by now, or their fate could have been decided by their anxious parents. But for now, they waited with bated breath for the ones fit for purpose. Were they to go for all and sundry, or rather stick to their tribe in a foreign land? Would the diaspora be able to deliver? If not, the same question continued to linger on: *Who will marry us?* This became a collective psyche among the many girls that the motherland had spewed out, not to mention the boys.

Meanwhile, Melissa's mum was trying to figure out how to respond to her daughter's question. This had to be done carefully and considerately. She began to speak looking at Melissa, "I have been thinking hard about your question. It is not that I was trying to ignore you, but this is not just about your life, Melissa, but the lives of many girls and boys in the diaspora. Such an answer requires wisdom, knowledge, understanding, and insight. This question has vexed so many over the years, and many lives have been ruined because of decisions that were not based on true wisdom. The pressure to be like others and get married has destroyed the young lives of men and women. To this day they live in regret and wish they had known better when they made these decisions."

Beatrice continued. "Become the person you want to attract. Strive to become the person you expect to marry you. You can never attract a loving person if you are not a loving person. You cannot attract a genuine Christian if you are counterfeit fruit and not the real thing." She stopped and pondered. She was not sure how to proceed. *Should she give her daughter a full lecture on how to find Mr Right or wait for her husband who seemed to be dying to respond, judging by his facial expression?*

This sudden outburst by Beatrice was not something that had come out of the blue. She had witnessed scores of cases and heard stories of young men and women in her locality who had been struggling because of decisions they had made without enough thought. Some had been lured into such decisions by veterans of the illicit trade who posed as wolves in sheep's clothing.

Melissa, in a way felt for her mum. She knew how much pressure her mum was under, knowing that most of her friends and relatives had already celebrated the marriages of their spouses. "Mum, Sorry if I have upset you. I know you mean well and appreciate what you have taught me over the years. I sometimes get confused. You know what I mean. I wish any girl could go for the man they want without breaking cultural protocol," Melissa sounded defiant as someone who really meant it.

"Melissa, why don't we give your dad an opportunity to chip in. He has lived a lot in his life you know. Well, I am assuming that he can be open enough to dig deep into his personal experience and let you know how he got where he is now. It's a bit embarrassing for me. The way God connected us was…" *suddenly Beatrice thought to herself. It's better to let sleeping dogs lie. What if TK decides to dump all the trash including his past relationships. How will Melissa take it? For now, it was enough.*

Melissa took up mum's offer and looking across where dad was sitting said, "Dad you haven't said anything. Who will marry me? You know about my relationship with Brian, how it floundered because of his past. And Tom did the same thing to me. I am now confused, and sometimes I wonder whether it will ever happen to me. I mean marriage. Anastasia is living in with her boyfriend; so are Lavender and James. Everyone seems to be doing it. I have tried to live right but look what is happening to me." Melissa started to become emotional as she narrated the stories of her friends who had done it the "abnormal" way as far as her parents were concerned.

TK was startled. He was already glued to the television, thinking that he had got away with it.

He could not hold his horses any longer. "Melissa, the Bible in Proverbs 4 verse 12 in the NIV says 'there is a way that appears to be right, but in the end, it leads to death'. For every decision we make, there is always a consequence or price to pay. It is therefore very important to reflect on any decision we make. Look at the pros and cons and then decide. Every day we make decisions. You cannot be flippant about it. You ought to be very careful, especially when it comes to deciding who will be your friend for life during the good times and the bad times," TK finally responded.

TK thought: *At least I have shared what is on my chest without thinking much about how his daughter or his wife were going to react. Such courage was rare. Once the words had been spoken, they could not be retrieved. But he felt that he had spoken sense. It was for her daughter to make the choice based on the facts on the ground regarding the person she wanted to marry. It was for her to consider the implications of a rushed decision and the fact that she would have to live with her choice for the rest of her life. Many had made bad decisions and they were either stuck in their relationships or they had decided to quit and do it all over again. He thought of the rates of divorce among young men and women, the broken promises, broken marriages, and devastated relations.*

He began to sense some fear and trepidation. This could happen to his Melissa, if they failed to carefully walk with her through the maze of possibilities. This was indeed a critical question to consider and answer. He thought how wise her daughter was to ask this question at this time in her life. How many young men and women were doing this? How many parents were prepared to listen to such a cry for help?

Suddenly, TK sat up and looking straight into his wife's eyes, held her hand and walked away.

"I suggest we pray my dear, said TK seating on the side of the bed –it was a short prayer– God help us to find the right answer, Amen."

There was no doubt Melissa had opened a pandora's box. Mum and Dad had to seriously address these concerns from their daughter. They were aware that their friends too were facing similar challenges.

CHAPTER 2
UNIVERSITY CHALLENGE

Meanwhile George Melissa's friend's son, had finished high school with triple stars in all the subjects he'd entered. Here was a genius in the making. He was the youth pastor's favourite and never missed a meeting. He was always paraded as the perfect example of a young man every girl in town should go for—until he met his match.

Charlotte was equally impressive but pretentious. Their friendship survived many attempts by jealous girls to sabotage it.

She was cute, although she was not as clever as George, her boyfriend. She was an average student but always there to impress George's mum. She was very polite and willing to chip in whenever she was asked to help. She kept her baggage close to her chest. She had shredded all her photos from a former boyfriend except one revealing photo, which brought memories of her past love life. When George surprisingly grabbed a pen under her armpit, a passport size photo fell off.

"What is that?" George asked, not thinking much of it.

"Come on George, give it to me. It is an old photo of my brother," her heart beating fast. However, much she tried to reassure George of who it was on that photo, it left George unsettled. One day, he decided to let go of those "evil" thoughts. *It's history,* he thought. *Let bygones be bygones.*

George never thought much about his relationship with Charlotte after the photo incident. They decided to forget the past and start afresh. In a few weeks, they would all leave for university. George opted for Forensic Science while Charlotte chose her favourite discipline, Robotic Science. Marriage was not on the cards until they had embarked on their lucrative careers. Nothing would deter them from fulfilling their long-life goals. Any thoughts about marriage would have to wait for now. They were in love, and that was enough for now.

Melissa had always looked up to these two from the time their parents lived on the same street, back in the days when they left the village to join others in the diaspora. This was one of the reasons why Melissa had joined the local church youth group. George and Charlotte had gained a reputation in the neighbourhood. Many parents teased their daughters for not emulating Charlotte and George.

Even Benjamin or BJ, who always struggled to give up the bottle could be heard muttering kind words for George and Charlotte in his tipsy state.

Melissa too was one of a kind; charming but serious, reflective and daring. She had an aggressive faith in God difficult to quantify. She never went into something without assessing the reasons why. She was mature for her age. It was no surprise that she sometimes played the loner in school. Peer pressure was hard to get at her. She was a misfit of some sort to her peers. Uninteresting is what some boys thought of her. Hardly did she mix with others. No partying or pleasure seeking. A bit odd for an eighteen-year-old girl in England. But then this seemed to run in the family from her mother's side.

Back in the village, her grandmother was well known in the community for moral absoluteness. She was trained by missionaries who insisted that she reads the Bible and goes to church for her sake. She had adopted values that would make her a feared girl by those who grew up with her. She was considered too holy for the common young man in the village. They admired her in a way, because she always insisted on the reasons why she should do something. Ironically many were wondering whether Melissa would ever be married. Melissa had always admired her granny and no wonder why she seemed to have her traits in her system. She wanted the very best for herself and this is the reason why she insisted on Mum and Dad answering her question.

She had attended many youth focus group sessions in church and in the community hall, but the facilitators seemed to skirt around the question of marriage. It was too personal for them to tackle. They had failed at it themselves and were in no position to give a satisfactory answer. Even the local priest struggled to give a genuine answer as he too married out of wedlock, after some discipline from the church for doing so. It was difficult to find men and women who were role models. This was no academic exercise. This was a lesson in life itself and the examples had to be genuine, borne out of real examples. No wonder why mum and dad had to take their time to address these issues in bite size chunks.

Mum decided to continue talking as she tried to make sense of a complex issue. She embarked on a long and winded advice that seemed boring., "Melissa don't forget that unless you change, nothing will change. What you desire for yourself, must be evident in you – Beatrice continued with the subject to Melissa's surprise – You must change to attract a changed someone in your life. This is the first principle that must govern your life. What kind of person do you want for a husband? What are the characteristics you want to see in someone? Do you have these yourself? You should work at improving yourself and you will, over time, attract the man of your dreams. There was a man in the Bible, who made a very profound statement. He said, 'how can a young man or woman, keep himself pure? By keeping the commandments of God in his heart.' This is from Psalms 119:10 NIV. Many regard this as the old-time religion, but it works. If you reflect on the teachings of the Bible, you will be wiser and you will protect yourself from those things that will want to exploit you into making the wrong decisions about your choices in life," Mum stared at Melissa as if to signal to her that she was done.

Beatrice was conscious that Melissa had switched off. Her mind was wondering a bit as her mum seemed not to hit the nail on the head. *Why is she not giving me a prescriptive answer, Melissa thought?* Her mind raced left right and centre,

"Come on Melissa, TK interjected, Do you have a boyfriend now? I say this because we don't want to discuss issues that are not relevant to you now unless if you want some information to prepare you so you for when the time comes. I mean a sort of preventative approach. I guess you are right. It is no good researching about relationships when you are already in it. In a way, I am glad you are asking this question now," TK smiled sheepishly.

TK sometimes seemed a bit confused. He was never methodical in his approach. He was a scatter brain. He spoke impulsively and gave little thought to what he had to say. His wife had always been the mastermind behind all their plans and strategies. She was organised and reflective just like her mother. She played her wife role very well. She was submissive and never raised her voice even when TK tended to slide off topic. She was a woman of integrity. And if Melissa was going to make it in life, she was in the right environment, a cut above many of her peers.

Melissa was already learning by example. She admired the way her parents interacted and resolved difficult issues. They sometimes disagreed over certain issues, but they were very sensitive about it, taking care that their children hardly witnessed any altercations. All this helped shape Melissa. She was very observant. And sometimes she hardly said a word, but just mulled over the things she saw. Like any child she was so anxious to know what her parents thought. She kept insisting for an answer to all her questions.

However Melissa thought; *life was more than just giving straight answers. It was much more complex than that. Sometimes answers could only come from years of experience, from constant failure but not* giving up. Unfortunately, some of the areas where people failed tainted lives. They would be marked for life. Therefore, Melissa was keen to avoid such tragedies if she could. She had seen some of her friends sink deeper into a sinking hole never to come back. If they did, they were bruised, and heart broken. She had to do the best she could. It was important for her to find as much information as she could before it was too late. It was not going to be easy, but some had done it successfully. Her mum was a living example. Not to mention granny. The more she thought about this, the more she gathered courage and the belief that nothing was impossible. Faith, she thought was known to move mountains her mountains! It was a matter of keeping on pushing, gathering information and being with those who had been able to overcome the obstacles along the way. Her associations in the future were crucial if she was to learn a thing or two about decisions that will last a lifetime. Here was an opportunity with mum and dad by her side.

The Prickles did not quite live in the neighbourhood, but hardly a week passed by, and they were at the sea front close by. They were close to TK and his wife. Old associations that stemmed from their time in the army, during the war of liberation. When TK flew into Gatwick on his first trip to the UK, he had problems with Immigration. As he was being interrogated, he noticed the bold part of Sam Prickles head and immediately recognised him. They used to call him the airport runway as his bold head kept on beating records as the longest bold head of all time! That was the last time that TK saw Sam until Open day at the school where both their children attended. It was a meeting of old friends and from that time on they kept in touch, hence Sam's frequency in Luton where TK lived.

Anita 's baby was cute, innocent and cuddly. While Melissa was already thinking of going to University, Anita, the Prickle's daughter, had hardly completed her GCSE's. She got pregnant at 16. This was a closely guarded secret. Even the pastor at the church did not know. She continued to take mass or holy communion. No one of those who knew about it wanted to bruise the peaches. They let sleeping dogs lie. Sam and Grace, Anita's mum had bottled this up for some time. Anita was a go girl, free and gregarious. She enjoyed life. Her Facebook page was very popular not to mention her Instagram and you tube videos. Here was "Miss Social media," a great communicator. Her party exploits became a sore in the eyes of her dad. There were rules in the Prickles household and if there was anyone to flout them it was Anita. She had a reason for everything. When she got her passport, it seemed like a passport to no limits. Her mum had tried unsuccessfully to remind her of God and how good girls were expected to behave. 'Mum, we are not living in your century, this is our century,' Anita would retort back, whenever a suggestion was made that she should slow down. To be fair, she was the only child and rather spoiled. Her world was insulated. School was an experience of a lifetime. Her village roots could not be compared to what she was experiencing now. The boys here were wild and inviting like ferocious wolves waiting to pounce on their next prey. She had never been schooled in the art of survival. She struggled to say no when her moral values were under threat. She never knew what these were and when she was introduced to the world of romance and passionate exploits, she gave in.

A few months before her GCSE exams, she complained of a tummy upset. She was spitting all over the place. Her mum noticed that from time to time she wanted to vomit.

"Anita are you alright? You look unwell dear. Is there anything I can do? Mum asked

"Thanks mum I am fine. Perfectly fine, "Anita responded rather upset that mum had started noticing something. This went on for some time and no one dared confront her with the big question. *What if she is ...,* Anita's mum thought. She let *sleeping dogs lie* for now.

Just a few days before she delivered her baby, Anita became very poorly. She was monitored 24/7 and at one time the doctor was concerned. Five minutes past midnight on a Monday Anita came of age. The baby screamed as soon as it came into the wide world. It was cry of relief!

"Well done, Anita, you were very brave. Some experienced mothers cannot gather such courage when they deliver," the senior nurse assured Anita. Anita began to sob quietly as reality now set in; a new life, new experience, and a brand-new baby boy to look after. Her mum had been by her bed from the time she came to the maternity clinic. Her only child had given birth to her only grandson. This was no time to think of who the father was. For now, she decided to enjoy the moment.

"Congratulations lovely, look how handsome he is". she smiled at her daughter who looked dazed by now and a little tired.

For the Prickles this was a bittersweet experience. They gave up blaming the war in Zimbabwe, the spiralling economy, and their decision to relocate. They knew they would struggle with these decisions for some time to come but this was now their new norm. They had to gather up some courage and take the bull by its horns. It was time to begin again. How they wished Anita had emulated Melissa but realised that the two were miles apart in character. Maybe they should have remained in Zimbabwe, but even there, girls like Anita still had children out of wedlock. But this did not stop the blame game, which continued unabated for some time.

George's new university was the best in the area. It brought together the best students from all over the country. The first week was very laid back as they went through induction into their new life at university. There was plenty to see and many of the new students wanted to impress. There were all sorts of organisations from gay groups to Christian Union groups.

For the globally minded there were classes in yoga, transcendental meditation, karate, and sumo wrestling. There was a hive of activity and for starters this was difficult to take in. George was into martial arts at school and played a bit of football and badminton. He had to decide what to go for as he had become a fitness fanatic. And then there was Christian Union, where they claimed to teach about life and how to survive when temptation comes roaring down your corridor! *This is going to be fun,* George thought.

"There are basic things that you really need to know about

life here at Uni," Gemma began to introduce her favourite topic, 'How to go through University and win'. This was one in a series of talks that Gemma always gave to the new students as part of their induction. Gemma continued- You need to have moral principles. You need to be able to use the word No appropriately. You need moral absolutes. These are key to your survival here. Otherwise, you can easily be side-tracked and end up discouraged and way off the mark. Many have gone through this and sadly were unable to complete their studies. Some even lost their faith in God because they were unable to stand for what they believed in. Don't say I did not warn you. I will give you some time to discuss this in groups of three".

Gemma was very effective. She believed in allowing students to share their views and come to their own conclusions about the challenges of life. This was a training ground to prepare the students for the next few years. It was going to be tough but unless they could articulate their beliefs, preferences, they were going to be easy fodder for the manipulative vultures that littered the campus. This was not what George expected. He was intelligent but not in this sort of approach to life. It took him by surprise that not only had he landed on planet academia, but more importantly on planet life where one desperately needed the skills to survive. He kept thinking about the three words: Moral absolutes, moral principles, and the word No.

George was not the only one caught up in the maze of youthful intrigues and the confusion of making the right decisions. The environment had become so hostile that it produced schizophrenic young men and women. This was indeed moral schizophrenia. Boys were caught between two worlds. There were men and women who were on the brink of losing control. Years of child and adult education did not provide life skills to enable them to navigate the maze of life. If this was happening to George a young man with an admirable background, what about Wilson and Kate disadvantaged youngsters who grew up with George.

Wilson and Kate lived in a very deprived neighbourhood not very far from where George lived. They had enough to eat alright, but life is more than food. Occasionally in their street you would see litter strewn across the road. This was no ordinary litter. Needles, empty plastic packets which looked like they had been ripped apart in a hurry. Just across the street where Kate lived was the home of two well-known teenagers. They abandoned school when their teacher reprimanded them for smoking pot. They left in a huff and that meant that they were now in the neighbourhood full time. This was a jungle and survival was of the fittest. It was a dog-eat-dog situation. The police continued to monitor the area and knew who to target if there was a disturbance. This became so frequent that at one time, their parents, the Mahambas contemplated leaving.

"How do you teach a child about life in such a neighbourhood, Prosper or PJ, Wilson's dad suddenly opened his mouth. I am fed up."

What a revelation! PJ seemed oblivious to the fact that while neighbourhoods cringe under the weight of delinquency, life still must be lived. Choices still must be made. Girls must be married, and boys still must marry. Circumstances will go on unabated, and it is the responsibility of citizens of planet earth to find their way through this quagmire. The question from our young men and women is still relevant. Who will marry me? In these situations, in such a neighbourhood, under all these circumstances. PJ thought *Our responsibility is to provide the answers. To be part of the change process that will ensure that a conducive environment is created that will make the impossible possible. It is a tall order.* PJ realised that he had just opened a Pandora's box. A can of worms. *These were questions that needed an answer. You cannot pass on the buck when dealing with life questions. It is the responsibility of everyone to take the bull by its horns and seek to address such issues. We are all part of the change process. When everyone becomes responsible for what is happening around them, there is a better chance of finding a solution. And it is true that young men and women are under pressure in real time. Every day they are targeted. They lose faith in life. They succumb to pressure and in many cases lose the moral grip and tumble headlong under the bridge of troubled waters! This is a fight all of humanity must win.*

It is not just a fight in the littered streets where Wilson and Kate come from. It is a fight in the most affluent streets, in the affluent homes, among the millionaires and billionaires. You will find derelict young men and women who have lost direction. They have lost their appetite for life. They have allowed themselves to fade and to lose hope. Material things cannot satisfy. Those who sought solace in relationships were not prepared enough and the marriages quickly turned into boxing matches where love was mistaken for lust and commitment was misplaced.

This was the neighbourhood experience Wilson and Kate lived with all their lives. They had to craft a new and forward-looking existence out of this seemingly depressing environment. They had to make choices. They had to discard the rear-view mirror of their lives and look ahead with hope and faith in the future.

A significant number of students during the first week of induction at George's University displayed confusion and amazement. What they thought about university was not what they were experiencing from those that had been there for some time. There was a new definition of knowledge. Academic prowess was not as impressive anymore. For the majority of those who had come from "decent" homes, University was a wild environment. They were failing to cope. There was a new kind of freedom. What was taboo on their street had become open for debate. What was preached as the truth, had become fake and prone to scrutiny. Their expectations were being questioned. In fact, this was not a safe place to be. You could not ask the serious questions anymore. Questions like 'Who will marry me 'because marriage itself was now being questioned and many were in relationships that raised eyebrows. They could afford to. They did not have to live on campus. They were in rented accommodation and the carnal in them suddenly went haywire. This was freedom. No parents. No pastors. No youth leader. Away from it all! However they still had to be accountable and responsible for their actions.

It was Gemma from Christian Union who demanded that students consider the implications of their actions whether at home or on campus. In fact, she emphasised the importance of life as a teacher and that every experience was a learning curve. While University seemed a confused place, there was still hope. Out of its corridors came out young men and women who became pillars of their communities steady and ready to help others realise their dreams.

When Charlotte experienced her love set back, she had a few regrets. She admitted she had made the wrong choice. She knew in her heart that what she was doing was wrong. That he was not the right match for her, but she overruled her conscience and took the plunge. So were the decisions of many over the years. But this was what Melissa wanted to avoid. She wanted to do the right thing. Her question was genuine, and she wished mum and dad would carry on their advice so that she could make informed choices in life. Tough but expedient. Unless she changed herself, nothing would change. She always remembered those words from her father.

TK's neighbourhood was diverse. Just across the road were the Ibrahim family, whose daughter Fahima graced the street with a smile that made all the parents wish their sons were married to her. Faisal, a young man of eighteen years was already enrolled at the local college when his parents arrived from Afghanistan. He too looked like a possible candidate for Fahima. The gossip was tense and many in the street seemed happy and contented about how life had treated them. It had been tough but challenging. Everyone, including Mr Brown, a true Englishman whose deep Oxford accent betrayed him even though he had spent most of his life in the British Civil

Service as a diplomat in Oman, Cairo, and Singapore. His daughter Beth, who lived in York was married to a Tichaona, a Zimbabwean whom she met at the American University in Cairo. She regularly visited her dad. James Brown was proud of his grandchildren, who seemed to spend most of their holidays with him since Marianne, his wife had died of colon cancer a few years back. On her death bed, she seemed to know that she had a few months to live. She asked Beth and Tich (short for Tichaona) to bring her grandchildren into hospital. The hospital made this visit an exception since kids were normally not allowed in. She hugged each one of the three and said a prayer for them. This was to be the last time. At her funeral, the Pastor reminded everyone of the need to count their days. This was the importance of living with intensity in a world where tomorrow was not guaranteed.

"Marianne was a wise mother, wife and nan. She prepared herself for life without her family. She enjoyed quality time with her grandchildren," the pastor went on. This was a moving funeral service. Many of Mr Brown's neighbours attended the funeral. Melissa and her mother stood at a distance trying to get a better view of the proceedings as the pastor was conducting the service. She would occasionally get lost in herself. Her imagination wondering far away from the funeral. She looked at Beth and Tich. She wondered how Tich had been able to marry Beth. And when the pastor talked about the relationship between Marianne and her son in law Tich she wondered if this was going to be her narrative too.

Here was a couple from different backgrounds happily

married and in love. *Who will marry me?* Melissa thought. Uncharacteristic of him, Tich began to sob loudly. He had lost a mother prior to marrying Beth. She died in a horrific car accident that left his dad paralysed. That is why he could not attend the funeral from the nursing home near where Beth and Tich lived. Marianne had taken the double responsibility of looking after her daughter and son in law's spiritual welfare. She was there for them and occasionally would go for endless car drives just to talk. Tich needed lots of encouragement and he had found this in Marianne. She was known for her deep faith. Even in hospital when she was poorly, she kept a Bible next to her bed. And because she found it difficult to sit up, she turned on her audio Bible. She could listen to whole chapters endlessly punctuated by music from her iTunes account. Her favourite song from the iTunes library was 'It is well with my soul', written by Horatio Spafford and composed by Philip Bliss. Tricia, one of the nurses who cared for Marianne in hospital spoke at the funeral. Her testimony touched many hearts. Unknown to Bob and the rest of the family, Marianne had become a source of encouragement and comfort to other patients in the hospital. She exuded a contagious smile that was radiant and spoke volumes about her faith in Jesus Christ. Early on when she was still able to walk to the toilet, she would stop by several patients and hold each one's hand and say, It is well.

It was late in the evening when Melissa and her parents got home. And all the way from Oxford, where Marianne was buried, Melissa kept thinking about what she had witnessed. She kept thinking about the question she had asked mum and dad many times. Now she seemed to have got part of the answer from seeing Tich and Beth. At least she was convinced it could be done. She kept all these things in her heart.

There was a time George struggled at University. He could not quite settle in as the culture was alien to what he was used to. He felt isolated except when he went to meet with his friends at the church youth club. This was his comfort zone. He could spend hours on end, playing badminton or in the gym where he heaved and sighed on the weightlifting corner. Occasionally he would get a text from his girlfriend, but these had become erratic. He kept pushing these thoughts away as he concentrated on his studies. But these thoughts kept nagging him. He occasionally had dreams where he saw her screaming at him. She had this plastic face that looked like it would stretch and shrink at the same time. The face was distorted, and the image became fuzzy. And then he would wake up again. He did not know that this was the beginning of a strain in their relationship. While she was a strong Christian, she was now under pressure from some of the girls at her university who seemed to know it all. They called themselves Christians but seemed to live odd lives. They were hypocritical. They were rather fake but adept at keeping their darker side at a distance from public scrutiny. But for how long, one wondered.

The Village hall in the neighbourhood where TK lived was a hive of activity most Saturdays. Either there was a birthday party or there was a celebration of some kind. This time Melissa was invited to attend a focus group discussion organised by their church. There had been many requests from the neighbourhood for the church to organise discussions on issues that affected the young people in their area. When word went around that brother Paul would facilitate the discussions, there was a buzz of excitement. He had been married for over five years and yet they still called him brother. He remained close to the young men and women whom he served during his years at the Redeemed Church. He was blessed with a wife who was beautiful and had a heart of gold. She was unassuming, always willing to step in when some girls showed signs of spiritual fatigue. And yet her love and passion for others had taken its toll on Tara. Was it not for a strong and loving husband, she would have curved in under pressure from not only young girls but the women of the night, whom she took turns to visit with her spiritual partners?

She was a member of Street preachers, who would walk the byways and alleys across town talking to commercial sex workers. Sometimes they would be mistaken for prostitutes themselves by unsuspecting men in posh cars, who were prowling around seeking whom they could devour. On one occasion, a car came screeching to a halt, someone opened the passenger door and beckoned the street pastors to come in for a ride. The man shouted obscenities the moment he realised they were not for the taking. It was this constant barrage of abuses that was beginning to affect Tara. Coming from the street well after midnight meant sleepless nights in bed as she tried to process what had gone on. She would kneel and pray, sometimes crying for the lives of these young women who had decided to become ready fodder for the men on the street.

It must have been prayers like these that eventually saw the convening of a focus discussion on the many issues that affected the young men and women in the neighbourhood.

This Saturday afternoon, the hall was packed. Young men and women from the Suburb and some from across town sat, stood and some milled around the hall, waiting in expectation for the man of the hour. The subject under discussion was too important to be missed. It seemed like everyone was seeking an answer to this fundamental question. And for Melissa, at last, someone had decided to tackle something which had taken ages for her parents to address.

Brother Paul was already standing at the podium ready to crack on. *He was a towering figure but handsome, with a crisp voice that went husky each time he wanted to emphasize a point. He was candid and did not beat about the bush. This was too much of a serious matter to skirt around the terraces. Many lives depended on it. Young men and women had ruined their lives. Many were on the streets because there was no platform to address these issues. This was the time. It was a defining moment. And for Melissa, this was an answer to prayer at an opportune time.*

Brother Paul began to speak with all eyes glued on him "There is no need to beat about the bush ladies and gentlemen. Yes, you have guessed it the big question we will discuss today is Who will marry me. It is not being addressed to me but You. Why don't you personalise it? Think of yourself. Are you desperate? Have you reached the end of your tether? Are you so let down that you have lost hope in the future? How do you identify your target? Who is your future husband? Who will you marry? How do you do the selection? What are your criteria? What things can go wrong in your selection? What are the long-term consequences of making the wrong choice? And if you have already made a wrong choice, how can you rectify it?" Brother Paul kept on splattering all kinds of scenarios.

You could tell from the faces of most of the young people that they were confused. It was too much. Their calm waters had been disturbed. You see, some were already in dodgy relationships. It seemed brother Paul knew what was happening to them. They were jittery, uncomfortable. There was emotional panic. Some felt uneasy. Some were on the verge of leaving the hall. This was not what they had come for just to be unsettled before the main talk. *Had they come to witness someone grave digging in their lives*, they thought. Even Melissa began to have her doubts. She expected neat answers, nicely tabulated. Perhaps a handout explaining how one could identify a partner to marry and then go for it. Not so with brother Paul. Like a bridge over troubled waters, he was there to help them cross it. In order to help them avoid the troubled waters below, he chose to be candid so as to avoid sinking and drowning. This was their only escape from the ferocious crocodiles that were a menace in the river of life.

Brother Paul continued, "Why should anyone marry you? What qualities do you have that will attract a possible candidate to want to hook up with you? Is what you want in the other person part of who you are? Remember like attracts like. So, this is where we need to start. Examine yourself, who you are and what you want to be and become. Remember nothing changes if you don't change- *Brother Paul did not mince his words. He was an action person. He believed in people taking responsibility for everything they did*- The buck stops with you. This is no blame game. Remember what the Bible says, 'Don't team up with those who are unbelievers. How can righteousness be a partner with wickedness? How can light live with darkness? What harmony can there be between Christ and the devil? How can a believer be a partner with an unbeliever?'2 Corinthians 6:14-16 NLT

Immediately after his heart-searching introduction, small focus groups were set up and dotted all around the corners of the hall. Some spilled on to the immaculately cut loan outside. It was a hive of activity.

The report back session was interesting, to say the least. Each group had come up with what they considered to be vital criteria for the man or woman they would go for. You could tell that this was done from the heart. Only one group tended to have lost the plot. They were petty and lacked seriousness of purpose. Perhaps they did not think that their contribution would make a difference.

Melissa's group was the first to report. When Melissa walked on to the platform, you could sense that she was a well-respected girl among her peers. You could hear a pin drop. She cleared her throat, and from then on, it was a serious delivery of the key pointers to look for in a man or a woman.

"Our apologies to any gays and lesbians, our group looked at marriage between man and woman, Melissa chuckled (*This apology was a surprise since this was not talked about when brother*

Paul gave the task to all the groups. It sounded strange, coming from Melissa. But not so. At the back of her mind, she thought of her little sister who, months before had phoned to say that she was a lesbian and was going through hormonal treatment. But no one knew up to this point. None in the group and in the neighbourhood. It was a closely guarded secret. Not anymore. Many would ask Melissa after this. She shrugged those thoughts off and continued with her presentation)

First, before considering whom to marry, it is important to realise that marriage is a long-term commitment. It is not something that we do as an afterthought. It is a sacrifice. You decide to commit the rest of your life to someone, a stranger with a different background. It is in fact a covenant you enter. It is a solemn promise to become one with the person. So, before anyone can make such a decision, one must count the cost. They must be prepared to face the challenges that marriage brings. There are many temptations along this journey, and one should anticipate them and prepare to meet them head on. So, we must first assess the situation and anticipate the risks involved before we take the plunge. You must make a commitment to yourself to uphold all that is needed to make the marriage work. It is this information that helps you to prepare yourself to be a suitable somebody who can attract another from across the fence to bring you together should you decided so one day. In our group we put the greatest emphasis on **preparation**. You must be ready for it. There are many things that you can do while waiting for the one destined to become the lover of your life.," Melissa paused.

Many faces were glued on her as she spoke confidently. It

was like she was beginning to understand the complexity of the question she had asked her parents from time to time. This was a revelation to her as she made the report. There was a glow in her face as she kept hammering the word lover of your life. *"Life has strange ways," she thought. All these years I have been seeking the answer to this elusive question. And here I am getting it in this hall." She thought to herself as she concluded her report.* Melissa forgot to realise that this was a deliberate strategy by brother Paul and his team to bring young people together so they could, through open discussion and scrutiny, answer their own question. It helped them own this enquiry and whatever answer they came up with, they hopefully would take it seriously. History was witnessing the birth of a new Melissa a new youth, and a brand-new understanding of the seriousness of getting married.

Melissa carried on from where she had left off. "So, when you look for someone to marry, you must remember that it is a LONG-TERM commitment, which requires lots of PREPARATION. In our group, we considered these words in detail. What is a long-term commitment? And when you make one what important things must you consider. How much will it cost you in the short and long term? What do you need to do? It is a conscious commitment. No one will bulldoze you into making that commitment. And should you be unsure of it, you can withdraw before you finally take the plunge. You should give yourself time to see if this is the right decision you are making. And if possible, seek advice from those who have travelled the same road before. We mentioned your name brother Paul in our discussions. This is not meant to embarrass you but everyone in our group wished they could make a similar decision to yours. Your example is great. And we also looked at other families within the community and in the church, who seemed to be struggling in their relationships perhaps because they made rush decisions.

Preparation as far as we were concerned was the key thing. As young people, we have all the time to develop ourselves. We must read and listen to others, observe great marriages, and correct things that are not good. These discussions should be part of our preparations. And as we meet at forums like this, we seek to change for the better. Thank you guys", Melissa walked off the stage to a loud applause from the young people.

It was clear that many of the young people were receiving mixed messages from society especially from the social media. It was very difficult to hold on to the truth. Or was there truth anymore. It seemed relative. It depended on the situation. And for those who had been brought up in the Christian faith, it was even more complicated. The Jesus they had been taught about who was loving but did not tolerate sin, seemed to have been watered down. The God who was loving as well as holy, was being made to be so loving that he ignored sin and gave it a new definition. Mistake. There was so much literature that fed into the minds and young hearts of boys and girls, young men, and women, that it needed spiritual discernment to know right from wrong.

Even Melissa began to appreciate that answers to her fundamental questions had become blurred in the environment in which she now lived.

Then it was George's turn to report on behalf of the second group. Their report was shorter than Melissa's group. They had struggled to come up with coherent answers to the dilemma.

However, George started off very confident. "Our report may sound controversial. We discussed the need for marriage. Is it important to marry anyway? What if one did not feel like getting married, or they had exhausted all channels. Was it important currently to talk about marriage when many young men and women were now cohabiting without a sense of the sanctity of the institution of marriage? (George's *group was made up of all sorts of young people. Some had never experienced a relationship with Jesus Christ. They were at the periphery of the kingdom of God. They were still searching and the only information that they had, came from their experience in the community. What they saw happening in families, at school, in the clubs and among friends they had grown up with.*)

We had to go back to the Bible to find the reason for marriage from the first couple God created. Our group identified four key words, vital to marriage and as important criteria to look for when one seeks somebody to marry. **Commitment, Transparency communication and complementarity.** Marriage as an enterprise calls for commitment from both sides. This is a lifelong project. One must view it that way. The reason many don't make it along the way is that they fail to count the cost of the commitment before they plunge into the unknown. Such commitment is not anchored on emotions, otherwise it will not last. It is not dependent on the advice of others, lest they short-change you in their advice. It is not dependent on what your peers say otherwise they can mislead you. It is an act of the will. It means being determined to commit oneself to the other person. It means constant communication with the God who initiated marriage in the first place. Failure to acknowledge that marriage is God's project for men and women, nullifies the very ethos of the institution itself. You can't have it both ways. Either you hold on to the sanctity of marriage before you embark on the project, or you walk into it hoping it will work. And in many cases, there is no guarantee. Commitment means singleness of purpose. A desire to make it; collaborate with your intended wife or husband (*It was becoming obvious that George's group had spent some time thinking about this topic. Theirs was a mature presentation, well thought out.*)

Transparency is equally important. The first couple in the Garden of Eden, were naked and yet that did not bother them. They could not hide anything. This is an object lesson on the importance of transparency for anyone who intends to embark on project marriage for life. As far as is possible, it is important that a 'no secrets' policy operates even before you get married. This is the desire to be open with each other and to be able to share the important things of life as an expression of your commitment to each other. Many of us young people get married but keep our secret closets to ourselves. And when these accidentally open during the lifecycle of our marriage, there is an implosion, and the relationship starts to disintegrate. We have a great opportunity to rectify this before we make a commitment to be with someone for the rest of our lives. And there will be many who would want to marry you if this is the position that you hold. It is human nature to want to associate with someone who is transparent and who will not cheat on them because they have nothing to hide. (*Brother Paul was already signalling that they were running out of time. Many young people were now absorbed into the report and looking forward to hearing more. George's group had touched a raw nerve. This was the stuff many young people were keen to discuss.*)

I will summarise one last point– George continued– I wish I could finish the whole of our report. Finally, we looked at communication. When God created Adam, he saw that it was not good for him to be on his own. I am sure God was aware that for there to be meaningful communication, you need two people. To communicate is a decision that anyone wanting to embark on project marriage must make. It is the glue that connects the two together. Many of us communicate with ourselves. Communication is two ways. And when you decide to marry or to be married, set yourself this important goal; that you will always communicate meaningfully with the other person so that you keep the wheels of marriage going. And what an opportunity to practice this during your internship as boyfriend and girlfriend. It must be natural. I am sorry we cannot finish our report for lack of time." George concluded

There was a deafening loud applause as some of the young people banged on tables and chairs. There was no better verdict. This was the beginning of a conversation that would continue buzzing in the neighbourhood. And for Melissa, an eye opener and a realisation that in life sometimes it is wise not to expect a single answer to a multidimensional question. This was indeed food for thought.

CHAPTER 3
THE ENVIRONMENT

Back at the university, George found himself stuck at the back of the hall not sure whether to proceed or not. Many had trickled outside after the most bizarre presentation on Space technology by a visiting PHD research student. He seemed overwhelmed by the number of very insightful questions from the students. He just could not manage them. As George walked towards the entrance, Helen spotted him from the back of the hall. Helen was cute and here she was, standing by the doorway about to leave. George was not just attracted to her, but she had this irresistible magnetic pull. In this her fourth year after internship, she was experienced in this sort of thing.

"George or am I not pronouncing your name correctly, she muffled his name in such romantic sound bites that George just wasn't ready for it. He walked towards her almost with his heart in his hand! "Yea, I am out of here now" he said trying to gather some courage as if he was in cloud cuckoo land. "Guess you are going to your room now," she said. She thought to herself... *I wonder what he would do if I followed him into his room? I know he is serious about life and is keen to protect his faith in Jesus.* You see, Helen had led many innocent men on campus by the leash. Some clever, some strong, but all vulnerable. The book of Proverbs in the Bible seems to clearly describe Helen's character:

> "Many are the victims she has brought down.
> Her slain are a mighty throng.
> Her house is a highway to the grave,
> Leading down to the chambers of death" Proverbs 7: 26 –27 NIV

George was lost, confused and vulnerable. He could barely gather sanity. He suffered memory loss for a moment and all that he had learnt from home and church seemed to vanish into thin air.

He struggled to unlock his room. She grabbed the keys from him. George apologised for the mess in his room as he did not expect a visitor this time of day. She comfortably slipped into the only tiny sofa in the room and mumbled a few words.

"Is that you mum on the phone? This late? Sorry for intruding", Helen said. She seemed very uncomfortable as she could not make sense of the conversation between George and his mum. The longer this went on the more anxious Helen became. Surely this was not going according to her plan.

George held tightly to his mobile phone. Mum did not normally ring late, but on this day she did. George tried to compose himself as he spoke to her. He carefully closed his eyes as mum started praying. He sat by the study desk and continued as if in a trance.

"Amen. Thank you, mum." George responded

"Same to you. Good night son." said mum as she put the phone down.

Helen was uneasy from the time George spoke to his mum. She shuffled from one end of the tiny sofa to the other. And as George continued with his eyes closed, she sneaked out of the room hardly saying goodbye.

George did not sleep well that night. He thought long and hard about what had just happened. The near miss, the emotional turbulence that he had experienced and how his mum had unknowingly come to his rescue past midnight.

While this was an indication of the environment that George and many young men and women lived, this was just the tip of the iceberg. George thought... *the "road to marriage was littered with many obstacles. No one was spared but everyone had to be prepared to face these many hurdles. It was clear from George's experience that character was of the essence. It was important to know where one stood and be able to stand by the moral absolutes that were the cornerstone of ones' life. It was not enough to rely on the odd phone call from mum to rescue one from the brink of disaster. There was need to make a deliberate choice of the way one wanted to go. A stubborn belief in those things that matter. A deliberate intention to achieve one's goal and not to be pressured by those around. One had to be able to shout the word "No" when appropriate and resist whatever temptation coming one's way. This was a tough call and remains a tough call. George had learnt it the hard way. While he had shared this during his report back at Brother Paul's group session, he was glad that he had now gone through such an experience and was the better for it.*

CHAPTER 4
THE CHOICES

There was a time Melissa struggled with many unanswered questions. This had now become an obsession. Many of her friends had thrown in the towel. Mandi was now a single parent with two children. Her boyfriend left her for another woman. Chengeto got married in the Cathedral. It was a lavish wedding. The bride's limousine was just impressive. The gown looked like it had landed from outer space with the glitter from her crown blinding the eyes. She even sang her vows and could have been mistaken for one of the celebrities at Glastonbury Music Festival! The marriage only lasted two years.

Such was Melissa's experience. And yet she remained hopeful. She kept believing. Her faith did not let her down. She remained patient. She believed that just as she was desperate to get married, there was someone out there who was too. And sooner or later, the two would meet.

TK, Melissa's dad, came from a very closed community. Many of the young men and women were taught to believe in their culture and identity. The world out there had to be treated with caution. They hardly mixed even though they were thousands of miles from there indigenous home. For them, the Diaspora meant that they could still create their own enclave where their culture and way of life would survive. The challenge was to build a wall around their culture so that it remained untainted. But they forgot one thing. Daily, their children were out there exposed to the real world in school, at university and at work. Who would ensure the preservation of their culture then? And the older people in their closed community were becoming an endangered species. But for now, these questions were not entertained. And meanwhile young men and women were under pressure to marry. But to whom if they had such a closed community mindset? Melissa had struggled with this for years. And now was the time to act.

Of all of Melissa's friends, Desiree seemed like the reflective type. She hardly said yes or no to something without giving it some thought. Like Melissa, she was mature for her age, being three years younger than Melissa. Her upbringing was very regimented. Her mother, having been one of the few women commanders in her platoon during the war of liberation showed her the way. She was one of a group of twenty-one girls who absconded from a tiny Boarding school in the Eastern highlands of Zimbabwe. They made it during the early hours of the morning, through thickets across a mountain steeped in the spiritual traditions of the area. Many had passed through its corridors in broad daylight and disappeared. The girls walked for miles until dawn. The rendezvous point was just three kilometres from the Mozambique border. They made it and for the next few years they were transformed into real freedom fighters. Desiree grew up in an environment where her mum knew the importance of discipline, resolve and commitment. Melissa appreciated her friends' character, and many times learnt a lesson or two on how to make decisions. She observed carefully how Desiree socialised and how careful she was on whom she took her fancy.

"You've got to know what you want before you make up your mind about something. You are special, and it's no good behaving like you are there for the taking," Desiree's mum would say to her whenever she seemed hesitant to take certain decisions. Many girls had fallen prey to boys with dodgy characters. They would sleep with the girls and dump them afterwards. That was what Desiree's mum could not stand. Why give in when you can easily say no. Why give in?

This was the in thing for many young men and women. Desiree's mum had gone through similar experiences. A handsome lad would pretend to be in love. They would fall in love and promise to get married. But very slowly and unknowingly they fell into a trap. It always started off after party nights. They would end up in his house. In bed. She would sneak out just before dawn to drive to her house, until both their consciences were seared. No more heart throbs. *If their friends at church do it why not them, they thought.* The desire to get married soon faded away. They found comfort in living together. Both their parents watched. It seemed justified. They had both learned the lesson and did not want their children to behave as they did. No wonder why Desiree's mother always took time to make sure that she put in a word to her daughter. She hoped and prayed that the future would be different from hers. And it was.

Since slipping away discreetly from George's room following his mum's embarrassing call, Helen had become wary of whom she took her fancy. It wasn't like her character was botched, but she was struggling to find her identity like everyone else. In fact, her dad was well known in the neighbourhood. Since the death of his wife, he took to doing acts of kindness in the community. He was not your kind of Christian. He prayed but was very shy when it came to talking about what he believed in.

Unlike George, Helen was born in the Diaspora. She had grown accustomed to the traditions and culture of her homeland. Her parents were more liberal than other parents from abroad. Her Latvian connections on her mother's side, sometimes bothered her. However, she had a strong personality but each time she wanted to establish a relationship with a bloke, she was misunderstood. She did not see why she could not be aggressive enough to lure a man she desired. She always felt like time was running out, and unless she adopted a winning strategy, she would miss the boat. The question, who will marry me, always lingered at the back of her mind. And her experience in George's room was a rude awakening. *How could George's mother pray with him about these issues? she thought. Were such decisions so critical that they needed God's intervention? Why couldn't one just go for it, without outside intervention? How can one know precisely that God has approved the one to marry?"* Helen was not alone in asking these questions. Young men and women were struggling to address these issues. And it seems that there were very few forums where these could be discussed candidly. This led to many men and women going for it without much thought. And the result was an increase in the number of failed relationships, suicides and failed marriages which only lasted a few years.

CHAPTER 5
A TALE OF TWO CULTURES

Melissa still remembered the focus group discussion at the Hall with brother Philip where she reported on behalf of her group. Serious issues were discussed. While her parents had not quite responded to her question, she had enough information to reflect on. She realised how difficult this process was going to be. Any decision that she was going to make would need serious contemplation and much help from others as well. In the end she would have to make her own informed decision and hope that this was the right decision.

Melissa had hardly finished tidying up when the phone rang.

"Hi, you are kidding me. Susan, where are you? What do you mean you are phoning from USA? You are kidding, right?" It was indeed a surprise. Her calling from the USA was not the surprise, but Susan's claim she had possibly found someone to marry her. The love of her life she said. Where is he from? Melissa asked.

"Mm. Iraq" she stuttered.

Melissa nearly fell over. "Don't joke about these things Sue.

What do you mean Iraq? You mean Iraq as in Iraq? Is your Geography up to speed. Sorry Sue I just can't get this into my head."

Thoughts raced through Melissa's head. *Susan her friend was born in the UK and her parents are from Zimbabwe. She had gone to study in the USA and now she was contemplating marrying someone from Iraq? This did not make sense. Why was Susan complicating her life like this? How did she come to such a decision? What would be the long-term effect of such a decision, Melissa wondered.* This was confusing. Melissa was anxious to hear from Susan, for example, how she came up with such a recipe for disaster?

Susan quickly interrupted, "Melissa, it is not what you think. He is such a gentleman. He speaks good English. Susan assured Melissa. Above all he loves Jesus Christ. That matters very much to me. I will have to tell you about it some other time to explain this weird decision of mine Melissa." Susan assured Melissa

"Yes, you must try and knock some sense in me Susan. How will you manage all this confusion? Couldn't you find some easier and less complicated relationship? What do your parents think about this? Melissa slowly carved her agenda into Susan's story.

Susan knew what Melissa was getting at. She knew the struggles her friend was having concerning marriage. Melissa had just turned thirty and suddenly it dawned on her that before long she would be forty years. She was racing against time. Many of her school mates had two, three up to four children. Some were happily married, some were not. This was not an ordinary conversation. Not just girl talk. It was serious business. And Melissa needed psycho-social support, otherwise she would break down.

"Melissa, we need time to talk about this. This was not an easy decision for me, Susan responded cautiously. I am hoping to fly to the UK sometime, and I would like to talk you through some of these issues. It has been a process for me. Fareed was really God sent. He too has been struggling with knowing the right decision concerning whom to marry. Their religion is very particular about such decisions. So, when we met and started talking about these things, you can imagine what we went through. But I am glad about the decision that I have made. Listen, as I said let's talk about it when we meet." Susan had captured her friend's interest in the subject.

Melissa now knew that this was serious. She thought, *hopefully this must have been an informed decision. No one would go for an Iraqi lad without having serious thoughts about it. A possible clash of cultures like this was not deliberate. Susan must have thought through this. And her serious Christian commitment must have been a factor in all of this. Thoughts raced through Melissa's mind. This may be an answer to what she has been struggling with. It may be possible to find a compromise in these relationships and in the end, get a better deal.*

"Listen Susan don't rush such things. Let us talk about it even before you come here. I will call some time. I am also trying to find my way when it comes to decisions about marriage. Maybe we can share experiences." Melissa spoke with confidence as she said goodbye.

Chapter 6
The Land of Opportunity

Ever since Tawanda was a child, she dreamt of living abroad. The magazines, films she saw at the local Grocery store fuelled this imaginary desire. Her year 7 teacher, a missionary from the UK, did not help her to realise how important and enriching her culture and environment was. She kept talking about her beloved country, her Queen, and the double decker buses that drove through the narrow streets of London.

And now here she was, at Heathrow Airport. Tawanda was asked a few questions at the immigration counter before she collected her baggage and was out in a huff. Graham drove her to the University residence and made sure she was settled in her room. She had never met him before. He was part of the Student Union welcome group. "Let me know if you need anything," quipped Graham as he slammed the car door before screeching off back to the airport.

It was not difficult for Tawanda to kneel and pray. She had a lot to thank God for. At last, she had realised one of her dreams. She pinched her hand as if to prove that it was her who was finally in the land of plenty. The prayer did not last long as thoughts of anticipation raced through her mind. She became emotional and after a few sobs, picked herself up. That evening the night was long. She tossed and turned and was woken by the sound of seagulls scavenging for food. She looked outside and alas, there was "white powder" all over. That was the first noticeable change. A hostile environment for Tawanda. That was the beginning of a long wake up call. What she thought about this land of plenty looked different and strange. It took her time to settle, to understand the language, the way things were done. Girls of her age seemed to behave like grown-ups. They dressed funny and were disrespectful. It was all confusing. She could not wait to explore her environment. Next stop was the beach, and to her horror, people looked half dressed! She could hardly look. *Was this the wonderful country that Miss Staines bragged about?* Tawanda thought. She dreaded what she had let herself into for the next three years at the University.

Graham was in his last year at university. His name was odd for someone born into a Syrian family. He looked Syrian but behaved like he was from the royal family. You would think he had been through elocution lessons that English butlers and maids went through before taking housekeeping positions. His mother was English. She had met his father at Oxford where they both studied Classics. His family were now in Damascus with their only daughter Fatima. Graham hoped to join them as soon as he finished University.

Tawanda was surprised to see Graham sitting two rows in front of her in Church. He seemed to be absorbed in the singing. Time and again, he would raise his hands, eyes closed and making "amen" sounds. The band seemed to belt his favourite songs. Tawanda was confused. She thought Graham would be either an atheist or a Muslim at best. *How could he be enthusiastic about Christian worship with his Syrian background,* she thought to herself. Graham was such a distraction to Tawanda that she didn't quite get into the service.

"Graham- Tawanda shouted as he dashed towards his car- Do you still remember me?"

"Oh, yes I remember you, Graham responded after they had briefly spoken about their first encounter.

"I didn't know you go to church," Tawanda said.

"I have been coming here for the last two years, Graham retorted. I will miss it when I leave," Graham spoke in a low tone voice giving the impression he was a committed Christian after all. The conversation seemed endless, and by the time they said goodbye many students from the campus had left. It was clear from the conversation that while Graham came from Syria, he was an active member of the church.

The two had not met since he picked her from the airport, the day she arrived. He pretended not to remember her, but inside his heartbeat jumped a few beats. For some reason, after he dropped her outside her residence, something happened to Graham. Here was a girl purportedly from rural Zimbabwe, with a reputation for moral uprightness and cultural etiquette. Even after their first encounter, he kept finding out more about Tawanda from those closest to her. He was impressed with what he gathered. She was brought up in a Christian family. Her mum and dad were career diplomats. While she was from the rural areas originally, she had been to many world capital cities in Africa where her parents were posted. She had flown from Luanda in Angola when she arrived at Heathrow. Graham was intrigued by Tawanda's background and her seemingly humble demeanour.

There was very little to do on campus, especially during induction week. Gazing from her balcony window Tawanda absorbed the crisp winter breeze that seemed endless. Even with the heating on, the place was just as cold. She had remembered to bring her old photos from Germany and New York of other diplomat kids like her dotted all over the world. She remembered her recent stint in Luanda, Angola. Hot, humid, and politically unstable. Her dad was involved with one of the churches in the city. They had to travel miles into the hinterland to help communities in need. This was one of her best experiences as she learnt to appreciate life from the other side. And whenever she thought about the plight of refugees in Syria, Iraq, or Yemen, it made sense to her. She appreciated how fortunate she was and what a challenge she had to be able to impact others who were in dire straits.

There was no doubt that Tawanda was now in her comfort zone. The UK was a far cry from her experience in downtown Luanda. This now resembled the glitzy streets of New York. Or close to it. She was paying international fees and her room was in the exclusive block reserved for Chinese students whom the University held in high esteem as they brought much income. The only downside for Tawanda was that she could not speak Chinese. Not that the Chinese could not speak English. When they were on their own, they preferred to speak their heart language.

"From where you come," Xi struggled to communicate with Tawanda.

"Oh, Tawanda rather surprised that Xi spoke to her for the first time.

Zim, I mean Zimbabwe," thanks for asking. Xi and many from China struggled to pronounce Zimbabwe. Fortunately, Tawanda had met some Chinese during the many diplomatic receptions she attended with her mum and dad when she was younger. Tawanda and Xi spoke at length about university, their families, the courses they were doing. Tawanda was impressed by Xi's appreciation of her and his gentleness. He came from a very poor background in rural China. However, because he was intelligent and worked very hard, he was awarded a scholarship to study at a reputable Boarding school in the nearest town. And when the local Council scholarships were offered to the school, Xi was awarded one to study aeronautical engineering in the UK. He was the only child.

The Christian Union was very active at Tawanda's university. They made sure that every new student was warmly welcomed and given the opportunity to realise their potential. They were careful not to impose their brand of faith to the incoming students. They always sought to present the message of Jesus Christ in a way that would allow students to make an informed decision. It was not always easy as they were competing with different groups, who were opposed to any mention of religion within the campus. This was a competitive environment for the "souls" of students. It left some students either excited or just negative and not wanting to take part in what was going on around them.

Tawanda sometimes did not understand why this was so. Her analysis, from the time she became a Christian, was simple. God was supreme. He created the world and all that is in it. All we ought to do, is to acknowledge what he has done and give praise to him. There shouldn't be any doubt about this. This was possible only through faith and not by rational argument. For her, Christianity was to do with faith and not rationality. Granted, events like the death and resurrection of Jesus were historical and did happen but it was not necessary to convince someone through argument. In fact, in such a land of plenty like the UK, she assumed that many people would embrace faith. She had read about missionaries who had come from the UK, including her teacher in High School. It now seemed that the nation had become a land of material plenty and not spiritual plenty. She hoped to be proved wrong as her time at University went on.

As Tawanda thought seriously about the spiritual state of her new-found home, she wondered how in the next three years she was going to cope. What kind of friends she would make, and as she struggled with one of her goals in life, what sort of person will she marry? This was still a long-term goal. Her present focus was to get through her studies, perhaps find a job and settle down. She knew her parents were for the moment praying for her to do well and eventually have her own family. Her dad married at thirty-two. Not at a tender age like his sister who tied the knot at twenty-two, but then she never went abroad. His choices seemed to be limited. After six years in the United States of America, he had a series of near misses. Not that there were no steady and beautiful girls. There were. Some very committed to the same faith as his. But the thought of going against the norm was difficult for Brine.

One of his cousins who visited him just before he flew to the USA, jokingly gave him a piece of advice. Leonard was far older than Brine then but in typical Shona tradition, he respected his young cousin. 'Eh, I hear you are going to be away for some time studying. Whatever you do cousin, don't marry a white woman!', laughing uncontrollably as he cycled past Brine's homestead. And all the years Brine was abroad, this advice rang in his ears. This was so not because he could not make his own decisions in life, but it was the conviction with which Leonard said these words at a young lad just about to leave home for the unknown, that mattered most. And even after six years in the USA, he could only find the love of his life when he got back home. He became caught in between two cultures and could not decide either way. Brine wrestled with this the last few days before Tawanda boarded the plane to the UK. Here was history repeating itself. Was it wise for him to throw hints at his daughter, warning her of pending dilemmas once she was on her own for such a long time? Should he share with her the advice that her cousin offered him? All he could do was to pray with his daughter asking God to take care of her. If he survived, so could she. If he was able to choose the love of his life, so could she, whether it happened abroad or at home. What was important was for his daughter to stick to the principles he had taught her from her youth. And these words of Jesus to his disciples in the Bible floated in his mind, "And surely I am with you always, to the very end of the age" Matthew 28:20(b) NIV *God is not limited by space, he thought. He is everywhere and he will help his daughter make the right decisions in her life. She was going into a land of plenty, of opportunity and she would be blessed in all areas of her life. Brine was echoing the thoughts of many mums and dads worldwide, who were in the Diaspora or whose siblings had left home for the unknown to seek education and jobs.*

CHAPTER 7
PEER PRESSURE

Ever since George had a near miss in his room from which he was saved by his mum's phone call, he was now street wise. He began to realise what pressure there was from everywhere for him to compromise. Pressure to give in to the dictates of others. How easy it was to be side-tracked from one's course of action. For a moment, he emotionally did not feel anything about his real girlfriend. His faith had been assessed, and his mother's prayer over the phone was a reminder of how to respond to pressure especially when you are cornered. He remembered the words in the Bible, 'Never stop praying' 1 Thessalonians 5:17 NLT. It reminded him of his other friend Dylan.

Following a similar near miss, in which he succumbed, the next thing was a phone call a few weeks later from his friend Fatima.

Fatima: "Dylan, guess what?" Fatima spoke with a shrill in her voice.

"What," Dylan dragged his voice as if he knew what was coming.

"I am pregnant. I did the test. I told you this would happen. If only you had listened."

Dylan coughed loudly as if he had been choked. He cleared his airway and hesitantly replied,

"Whose is it? and why are you telling me?"

Within minutes the impact and the consequences of both their decision was becoming evident. Not for now but for ever. This incident made George to realise how important it was to think through one's decision. To take responsibility even before the decision is made. To know what one wants and to make sure that it is realised as per plan. He was now wary of peer pressure and how to respond to it.

So many questions kept flooding in George's mind as he thought seriously about the pressures he had just gone through. He kept thinking of Dylan's dilemma, how it happened and how he would have to live with the consequences for the rest of his life. Not that he would not want to take care of the baby, but he had no means to. This was not planned, and he was not prepared for it. George began to realise how easy it was to succumb to peer pressure. He contemplated about the best defence against peer pressure. *Whom do you learn from when it seems everyone does the very things that can lead you into trouble?* Even if, in the case of Dylan, he should have been prepared for it, how would he do it. George had many times gone on the internet to find out the best way to sort one's life. He was seeking to find out what it takes to be able to one day meet someone who would be the ideal candidate. He had spoken to many older young men who were married. They too seemed to fumble through the answers, and judging by their choices, they were unsuitable counsellors. And then there were those who were pessimists from the start. They relied on the great myths about the state of play among young men and women in the community and at universities and colleges. He remembered some of these myths that were being thrown around by many at the campus:

You will never find a man of integrity today. Many of the boys are of dodgy characters and are cheats. No one is perfect in this world.

Honest Girls are hard to come by. They are either fake or pretending to be who they are not.

It is a waste of time to look for a girl to marry at colleges or universities. They can be very dishonest

George was quick to conclude as he thought: *The world keeps on changing. The old values seem to be neutralised by what is happening. It is becoming very difficult to make the right choices concerning marriage. We all need new skills and the correct tools to use to help us make informed choices. The resources are plentiful if only we are willing to look for them. For those who have a faith in God, guidelines are tabulated in the Bible. There are various books and other resources that we can use to help us take the right course of action. Here are some hints:*

Are you the right candidate for marriage? What characteristics do you have that should attract the other person to want to make you their preferred choice? Does your character have substance? What makes up the real you? What skills and talents do you bring to the table? Are you adaptable and can you accommodate someone who is not your type? Are you able to deal with raw material and make it into a finished product that can be usable and value for money?

Is it important to consider the parents of the person whom you want to marry? What if they do not approve of you because of cultural differences. How do you go around this challenge? How much should you listen to your peers who say it doesn't matter if you are in love. What may be the long-term effects of such a relationship? Or is there any effect?

This was George's monologue. It was inconclusive and inconsistent. He was left confused but at least he felt he had time to reflect on some of the fundamental questions that keep knocking on every young person's door. He remained resolute after his experience with Helen. He resolved that he would not only consult himself but refer to the faith that his mother held on to over the years. She did not allow the storms of life to tamper with her core values. She had learnt from the time she attended her first Christian meeting the importance of holding on to certain moral absolutes– honesty, integrity, faithfulness, purity, and truthfulness. These had carried her all the way to her honeymoon, where she could look her husband in the face with a clear conscience. It defined who she was and what she had been up to until now. There seemed no better example for George than his mother. And if he was to learn a thing or two about making choices, he had to start from home.

George's mother did not realise the impact her phone call had, not only on her son but on his girlfriend. It would not have mattered much if George's conscience had been seared, but it was active and responsive. His heartbeat became the policeman on that occasion. And for his friend, fear was unleashed in her because of what she knew from her parents and the many Christian friends with whom she sang loud hallelujah's.

George's mother rarely drove to pick him at the University. It was always his dad. He loved it because on the way he would pass through Alton Towers to meet a friend who was now the Operations Manager of one of the local companies. On this occasion, he went down with man flu. As she drove past the Student Union Building, George spotted her. His heart sank. This was unexpected. And there was no one else in the car. A quick replay of his phone conversation with mum, the prayer, the girl and all what it meant, cast a shadow over what was supposed to be a three-hour drive to Slough, near London. And yet he had faith in his mum and felt that this could be an opportunity to find out the answers to some of the questions he had been battling with. Faith overcame fear.

"Mum, can you reverse the car closer," George beckoned mum as he prepared to load the heavy suitcase into the boot of the car.

"Tell me when to stop, I can't see very well from here, she spoke as she slowly manoeuvred the car. Usually when dad drove up, he always went to George's room for the annual "inspection." Not this time, as mum was in a hurry to drive back. So how is uni. Is everything alright? Have you been going to the Christian Union? Are you still praying with your girlfriend? Mum continued to fire the questions. It was for George to pick and choose the ones he was comfortable with first. Mum continued her conversation, "You must be careful son of peer pressure. There are people who can lead you away from God. Girls. Boys. And if you cannot stand on your two feet, you will be swept away. I am not saying that is what you are doing. I am only talking to you like any mother should."

This was a difficult start for George, but he was patient. He knew that his mum meant well. This salvo was not meant to destabilise him but to reassure him of her love for him.

Her previous experience with her brother left an indelible mark on her. She always feared that this could happen to one of her children. Although George and the other children had generally been obedient kids, at the back of her mind was the nagging feeling, "what if". Agrippa her youngest brother, who did not do well in school, left home for the UK in the 70's. He was fortunate to receive a grant from the British Council together with many Zimbabweans, Indians, and Mauritians. After three years he graduated from University with a second-class honour's degree. It was not difficult for him to get a job back home as he had connections at the Ministry of Science and Technology, where his former A level teacher was now the Director. This is when the trouble started. He met a young girl. She looked promising and seemed to be the ideal wife. Their marriage was the talk of town and within a few weeks after their honeymoon, they were the envy of many couples. She was involved in the local church but after she had her first child, trouble started. He did not seem to want to be near her. He would come home very late and give the excuse that he had been with his friends. Several attempts by their marriage

Counsellor to resolve the issues, seemed not to work. It now became a marriage by proxy. And before long, Agrippa took to drinking, clubbing. He began to slide towards the precipice. All along he had started planning for a repeat stint in the UK. He felt like he was now a prisoner. No one seemed to understand him. He yearned for freedom. And on the 1st of August 2004, he bade farewell to his wife and relatives who had come to see him off at the airport. Claris, his wife, and their young daughter looked on as daddy, climbed the steps on to the aircraft. Claris was relieved somewhat that she was going to be free from the abuses that she had suffered during her short years as Agrippa's wife. She was however still going to miss him.

George's mother had never discussed this with any of her children. Every time her brother came to visit them, she glossed over it with jokes about him and how he had been successful in his career as an engineer. In fact, she hailed him as an example to follow. And yet, deep down she hurt so badly.

Agrippa kept in touch with his young family. He would phone late at night to find out about his daughter. At first, it looked like things were getting back to normal. At one time, you could hear the two of them laughing and joking over the phone. While theirs was not a perfect marriage, yet they tried hard to communicate regularly.

"Mum is Uncle Agrippa and his wife coming for my graduation? George asked as a distraction from the myriad of questions mum was asking about University. He wanted to avoid any questions regarding his girlfriend.

"He is coming on his own, unfortunately. Auntie Claris

and Gemma have decided not to join him in the UK. He says he is bringing a friend. Heaven knows what sort of friend he is bringing if his wife is not coming. This was just what George's mum did not want to talk about. She knew that once George asked a question, he would make a follow up, especially if he was not satisfied with the answer. George, can you switch on to Radio four, it's news time", she made the request not because there was anything particularly interesting on the news. She dreaded explaining to George how Uncle Agrippa and his wife had become so hostile to each. How he was in the company of another woman. And there were rumours that he had married her without his first wife knowing. The whole episode was complicated. It left George's mum torn between support for her daughter in law and her brother. To complicate matters further, he was planning to marry in church and wanted his sister to support her with her family.

"Why is auntie Claris not coming. George asked. Doesn't she have a visa? Surely uncle can apply for one. The Immigration people hardly deny someone's wife and family a visa to join their husband. Besides there are plenty of lawyers who can invoke Article 8 of the European Convention on Human Rights." George was genuine. He had great respect for his uncle. He was his hero.

"We shall see," his mother quipped. The rest of the journey was taken up discussing life at the University, George's involvement in the church and some of his dreams and ambitions for the future. And George looked with glee as the 50-mile road sign showed on the bend just before the home stretch.

He was happy that no real issues of personal concern to him had been raised by his mum on the way. He had escaped this one and he would need to be careful. He knew, however that while he had just escaped from the fowlers snare, everything was transparent before the God, he believed in. He could not run away or hide from him. He had to take responsibility for his actions if he was to become somebody to be admired. This was food for thought. For now, he had learned his lesson.

Such peer pressure George was under, was the norm in the Diaspora. Many young men and women had succumbed to such pressure that they lost their identity, their character. Many who frequented churches were no different. Some went there in the hope that they would catch an unsuspecting young man or woman to marry. There was now a desperation among the young people. Some of their parents too were showing signs of spiritual fatigue. They were getting on in age and the desire for grandchildren was unbearable. There was a realisation that they could die before they witnessed their children's marriages. Instead of giving their children proper advice concerning their character and the need to wait upon the Lord for the right man or woman, the opposite was true. They mumbled through and failed to deliver. They too were under pressure.

No wonder Melissa's parents could not answer a straightforward question from their daughter. All she wanted to find out was what her parents thought about marriage in such a hostile environment. The difficulty was making an informed choice in a world where even the definition of marriage was under reconstruction. How was it possible to make the right choice in a community where role models were becoming an endangered species? And yet you still found many young men and women tying the knot and living happily ever after. What was their secret? Melissa was not alone in her quest for an answer.

CHAPTER 8
GO FOR IT!

Melissa never forgot the focus group discussion she participated in when brother Richard brought his entourage at the Church Hall. The fact that she was one of the presenters made it easier for her to remember what went on. She kept the notes on her iPad. And many times, she would bring up the topic with some of her friends, as a way of gauging their position on this matter. Melissa was a voracious reader. She was an Amazon Prime member where she could order books without paying for postage. She subscribed to a variety of magazines especially those which addressed marriage issues. Her legal background helped her analytical mind to forensically sift through different genres of literature. She was not your run of the mill solicitor. She was successful, enthusiastic, and displayed a strong faith in a God she believed could take care of everything. She was sought after by many clients and her Law firm gained a great reputation in the West country. But at thirty-five, marriage remained elusive.

Melissa realised that there was no formula to having a successful marriage. Picking the right man was never impulsive. As brother Richard had said, one must work at it follow the guidelines that God has given and doggedly abide by them. She was reminded of the Bible story of Isaac and how Abraham instructed his servant to find a wife for Isaac. Melissa went through this story and was surprised at the detailed plan the servant adhered to before he could convince himself that he had found the right girl for his master. This was serious business because it was to be a long-term investment. This is the story from the Bible that later became a marriage partner template that Melissa and many others took hints from:

"Abraham was now very old, and the Lord had blessed him in every way. He said to the senior servant in his household, the one in charge of all he had, 'Put your hand under my thigh. I want you to swear by the Lord, the God of heaven and the God of earth, that you will not get a wife for my son from the daughters of the Canaanites, among whom I am living, but will go to my country and my own relatives and get a wife for my son Isaac'.

The servant asked him, 'What if the woman is unwilling to come back with me to this land? Shall I then take your son back to the country you came from?'

"Make sure that you do not take my son back there," Abraham said. The Lord, the God of heaven. Who brought me out of my father's household and my native land and who spoke to me and promised me on oath, saying, 'To your offspring I will give this land - he will send his angel before you so that you can get a wife for my son from there. If the woman is unwilling to come back with you, then you will be released from this oath of mine. Only do not take my son from there'.

So the servant put his hand under the thigh of his master Abraham and swore an oath to him concerning this matter." Genesis 24:1-9 NIV

There are many who will find this story useful as a tool for use in determining who to marry. Melissa thought long and hard over this. *She thought of the gravity of such a decision involving God, the importance of identifying someone with a sincere character. Someone generous, beautiful, and culturally acceptable. The importance of tabulating before God what kind of a person one is looking for. Melissa's parents had found this overwhelming. They had helped her the best they could, but she was to make the final choice based on what she believed her God was saying to her.*

And while Melissa enjoyed listening to those who claimed to have found the secret to marriage and read all the literature concerning this, time seemed to be fleeting past. Soon she would be closer to the forties club. Then her possibilities would be limited regarding children, career change and all sorts of decisions relevant to her age group. But she could not push Keith to make a serious proposal. She could not drag him into marriage if he was still not comfortable about it. In any case he had not asked her. This was a strange situation. You see, Melissa and Keith had become closer than the closest buddies and no further. They shared many interests apart from their love for Mental Health Law. While they worked for two rival Law firms, that was the end of the rivalry. They were committed to the same God and on many occasions, could be seen on the High Street distributing Christian pamphlets. Many rumours were doing rounds. Either they were secretly married, or they were gay. Why were they not getting married then? No one had seen them kiss which meant nothing was amiss. And yet all this was putting pressure on the two. They knew what to do, but none could take the first step.

Not for long. Keith was two years older than Melissa. He was an Oxford graduate who was one of the best students the Law school had produced for many years. But he was down to earth, unassuming, and very polite. Perhaps his belief in God made all the difference. He was the vice president of the Christian Union and had represented the University at many international conferences. He had friends from across the African continent, Japan, and the USA. His father was the Executive Director of one of the Oil companies that had lucrative contracts in the Middle East. And when Keith and his sister Theresa were young, their father would travel with them on his business trips. Their mother died when they were very young, and dad never remarried. Following their mother's death, Keith and Theresa were put into Boarding School from an early age and dad would only see them during school holidays. It was difficult, and yet his life revolved around his two children. Occasionally their nan would take them for a few days but only when this was convenient to her. Keith was always aware of his background. And although he could hardly remember his mum, he still felt the warmth of her embrace. This must have had an impact on his character. That warmth seemed to colour his conversation and his general deportment.

Melissa had taken notice of this. She was impressed by Keith's humaneness.

He was a genius but wise, intelligent but caring and above all had an infectious smile that seemed to always communicate hope. He was not a saint, but a sinner covered in God's love. A good Christian man, one could say.

Keith's dad's birthday was on a Wednesday. Keith had to travel all the way from Cumbria to the Southwest after work, about ninety miles. And because Melissa worked in Birmingham, Keith promised to see her on his way home. Melissa suggested that he passed through her office to pick up a little something for his dad for his sixtieth. Driving down the motorway Keith, for some reason kept thinking of Melissa. He had been through some relationships before and some aborted because it did not seem right. Others because the girls were downright unfaithful. One was tragically killed in an accident. Now here was Melissa, whom he appreciated and had good times with, and felt close to her. He had already bought his dad a birthday present. But he thought, *what present could beat the news to his dad that he was in love!*

When he got to Melissa's office, it was business as usual as she quickly handed him the small present.

"Thanks Melissa. That is very kind of you, and I am sure dad will appreciate this." *Keith paused, as if something had blocked his mental vision. He held Melissa's hand and could not let go. Melissa looked paralysed and before she could ask what was happening.*

Keith stammered, "Melissa, I know it's a bit strange to say

this now, but I. I … can … you … will you marry me"? he began to sob? He had never said these words before and for some reason he felt his mother's love warmly embrace him. It happened so fast that Melissa did not know how to respond. She could not confess that she too had been feeling the same for a long time. She thought about his dad, her parents, brother Richard and what this could mean to all those who had been thinking about her as she waited patiently to find someone to marry.

"Are you serious Keith, she asked. Not that she wanted a different answer. All she wanted was a confirmation that this was it. The beginning of a new chapter. They embraced heavily. Sat down and Keith had a few minutes to pray. After the prayer, Melissa confirmed," Yes Keith, consider it done, I want to marry you too. There was a smile on Keith's face. They both giggled. He had to quickly rush back to his car and started driving down the motorway. Now he had three presents for dad! Keith looked forward to introducing Melissa at his dad's birthday party in a few days.

As Keith's dad was escorted towards the hall, the doors flung open and the hall was packed with people all singing, Happy Birthday. By the time he was escorted to the high table, this was too much for Keith's dad Brine. He spotted his late wives' sister Ivanka, and her brother and many from his church. For a moment, he froze with emotion. Flashes of his late wife, the good times, the wish you were here thoughts, all wrapped into one. They kept singing, and some ululating.

At the high table, Brine recognised all those seated except one beautiful, well dressed tall young lady. She kept smiling sheepishly at Keith's dad. Melissa's heart kept pounding as she did not know how to respond to this. She had never met any of Keith's relatives, friends. *How would Brine respond to being introduced to his son's girlfriend of twenty-four hours ago, she thought.* The Master of Ceremony had already begun the introductions. He welcomed the birthday boy, Brine and those who had graced the occasion. Many had travelled long distances, included Ivanka who had flown all the way from Australia.

"Dad, this is Melissa a friend of mine," Keith quietly whispered to his dad.

"Oh, hello Melissa, good to see you," Brine responded with a smile. Keith had made similar introductions in the past and Brine did not take special notice of this introduction.

The party went on until midnight and was a special night for Brine. He had joined the 60's club! But something had left an impression on him. The girl that his son introduced to him was different from the other girls he had introduced to him before. Not only was she beautiful and well dressed, but she was also black and beautiful. He did not want to think much about this. Besides, if this was a serious relationship, Keith would have said so. She could just be a colleague from work, or a friend of a friend. Nothing serious.

CHAPTER 9
THE STRUGGLES

Monday morning when Melissa got to the office, her desk was as she had left it except for one thing. She was not the same. Friday, Keith was just a bloke but now she was seriously thinking of him as the man she had been waiting for. Not only that. She had to deal with the possible fall out from her parents, peers, and this cultural thing that kept peering on every Zimbabwean door. *But her faith was strong and beyond culture, she thought. Surely this should not affect the decisions that she makes. She was not there to be a people pleaser. This was a reality she had to deal with now that God had led her to the man she was convinced was kept for her before the beginning of the world.*

What a journey! Melissa was very organised in her mind. She kept a Vision Board in her bedroom which highlighted all her dreams, goals, and desires. She had done well so far in accomplishing some of her goals, but the marriage vision had eluded her for a very long time. Now this was it. The challenge was to make sure that her dream wedding, the children and all that happy families are made of became a reality.

This was a different Monday for Melissa. She struggled because in her mind the personal kept invading the professional; besides

Keith did not phone. She thought that he would check on her especially after what happened at the weekend. She struggled with this negative thought but had to remind herself that Keith was just a friend for now. She did not expect him to jump on the love band wagon. He was a man of character who would not rush things. *But a phone call would have been appropriate. Never mind, she thought.*

Keith stayed the night with dad and a few relations who had come from afar. It was a family weekend like they had never had before. The auntie from Australia took her relationship with Jesus very seriously. She is one of those who had promised to pray for Brine following the death of his wife. She was very close to Keith and his sister and drummed hope in them even during the time they mourned the loss of their loving mother. And for her the birthday brought memories of what could have been if her sister was still alive. Ivanka was keen to hear from Keith and her sister. During the birthday she had noticed, although Keith had shied away from introducing Melissa to Ivanka, that Keith had brought a friend. However, she did not want to bring it up during the party.

"Who was that girl Keith who sat at the high table with you," Ivanka asked. She quietly threw the spanner in the works, shattering the peace that seemed to prevail in the house.

"Oh yes, I meant to ask as well," Brine interrupted as if surprised. He seemed to welcome the introduction of this sensitive topic. Many questions raced through Brine's mind at the table when he was introduced to her during his birthday. Then he thought, *Where was this girl from? What was her background? Were her parents in the UK or she was just here to study?*

What could this mean if Keith decided to be serious with her. Was he prepared for an intercultural marriage? He had lots on his mind. He thought of the potential grandchildren, his relations, and their attitudes.

There was a long pause before Keith, showing great confidence replied, "She is my new girlfriend, my friend for life from now on. God gave her to me on Friday. Well, I mean this was when I popped the inevitable question to Melissa"

This was a stunner. It gave everyone little room to manoeuvre. This was a given. A decision beyond counselling or further comment.

Auntie just smiled. "Thanks Keith, I just wanted to know. I am sure we will see more of her in the future. And I will certainly pray for you two as you journey together." But Brine felt that this was not the appropriate setting for him to make a comment. His questions and concerns needed more time and a conducive environment. For now, this was the barest information that had been provided by his son to his auntie, and not for public debate. He kept everything to himself until another opportune moment.

One person Melissa was keen to talk to was her friend in the USA. Last time she called she dropped a bombshell saying she was contemplating marrying someone from Iraq. Then Melissa was surprised and wanted to know more about how it happened and how she thought this was a match coming from heaven. She could not understand how Sue could fall in love to someone with a Muslim background while she came from a country steeped in the Christian faith. Her friend had promised to talk about this when she came to visit the UK.

Melissa then never dreamed that she too would now be in a similar predicament.

The decision to accept Keith's proposal was not worth thinking about for Melissa. Here was a question she had waited for all her life suddenly popping up from nowhere. But now it was time to reflect. It was no longer a fairy tale episode like Alice in Wonderland. Keith was Caucasian, she was black. Keith was the crème dela crème of aristocracy, she came from a village in the far-flung sticks of Zimbabwe. Judging from the guests at Keith's dad's birthday, his relations were global citizens, all well to do and significant. Her only global family was her mum and dad and a sprinkling of relations in Dubai, USA and Botswana! This was the reality. Everyone at the party went out of their way to accommodate Mel. They were deliberately restrained in the type of questions they asked her for fear of embarrassing her. It was hard trying to navigate the murky waters of this relationship. Not that Mel minded then. Now was the time. She tossed and turned. She tried to read the Bible from her mobile. She said a prayer and still she could not sleep. And yet deep down she knew she had made the right decision. *She thought, other issues were peripheral. What mattered was Keith's commitment to her. Besides, it was a relationship between the two of them. There were no third parties to this relationship. Why should she bother herself about "significant others" who were not part of the equation? Culture, class, were important but not crucial. He loved her, she loved him and that was all that mattered most.*

Keith had already booked the table at the restaurant where they were to have an eyeball-to-eyeball dinner. The dust had now settled, and it was time to talk business, affair business. This was the first time they were to meet properly after the decision to become bosom friends.

Melissa looked prettier than ever. She walked in dressed in a silhouette dress that flowed gracefully to her knees. She put on mild make up as there was no need to impress. Strange, she had come in her own car a P registration that her uncle at church gave her as a present after qualifying as a lawyer. Keith stood tall and elegant, the product of a spoiled childhood. He wore one of his favourite maroon casual jackets and, with a broad smile tenderly shook Melissa's hand. They were like two teenager's meeting for the first time. The conversation went on and on and by the time dinner was served, they had made real progress.

"I didn't know you had a serious girlfriend before. What happened to her?" Melissa asked.

Keith looked uncomfortable, but he narrated to Melissa what happened. A tragic story which Keith had always avoided. Melissa took it in her stride. She showed her maturity.

She clasped Keith's hand and hesitantly said, "I will be there for her. You make me feel special Keith. She may not be around, but you are and that is all that matters."

"I love you Melissa, and I meant it when I asked you to marry me the other day. It is not going to be easy, but I promise, with God's help we will pull through," Keith slowly ploughed into his plate as he spoke, eyes fixed on Melissa. Here were two young people who had a history but who were, it seems, being rewarded for their patience.

CHAPTER 10
LOVE ACROSS THE ATLANTIC

Susan wasn't aware of the few students still at it in the lab. Experiments were not something she looked forward to. For some reason, she looked across the room and her eyes caught Fareed's. She quickly focused on her work, but something had registered in her mind. She coughed as if to clear a frog in her throat.

"Are you ok", Fareed had noticed Susan.

"I am alright, thanks", she answered politely.

Fareed walked towards her and quickly introduced himself and left. And that was the beginning of their long relationship.

Susan was not sure what had happened. This bloke, Middle Eastern in complexion and handsome had just walked into her life somehow and she knew something had happened. It's not that her heart went boom, but she knew. It was the tipping point. She prayed that she would once again come across Fareed. *What were the chances in a campus of nearly three thousand students? She thought.*

In any case, she had so much on her plate; the exams, visit to her uncle in Florida on her mother's side and just hanging around with the sisters she had befriended since coming to university. Besides there was a possibility of mum and dad paying a visit to the USA courtesy of the parish church where she attended. All these things occupied Susan not to mention the never-ending discussions she always had with Josephine, her roommate.

Sunday was always a busy day for Susan. And this one was no different. She picked two other girls on her way to church. She then drove to pick a fifty-year-old widow whom she had befriended during her first days at University. She went to a boot sale once and while looking for something to buy, bumped into this lady struggling to carry the piece of furniture she had bought. Susan, because of her upbring could not leave her but helped her carry the furniture to her car. That was the beginning of their relationship. And from time to time, Susan would be invited for tea and ended up in the same church with Auntie Grace, as Susan called her. Culturally, Susan could not address her on first name basis as this was unheard of where she came from.

On this Sunday, the church was packed by the time they went in. There was a lot of joyful singing. Many students frequented this Episcopalian church. The pastor was Caribbean and tended to attract many from different countries. There was loud singing, ululating, drumming. It was a hive of music vibes and rhythms. It made Susan feel at home. There was a sprinkling of hallelujahs' right across the church. It was a Youth Sunday. The whole programme was planned and run by young people some from the University and others from the Hood. There was always an expectation of great things when the young people were in charge. Rev Stanley was there but not to be seen. He believed in letting go and passing on the responsibility to the young. He had this legacy thing he always talked about. *When I pass on the baton, it's for real.* And this day was no different as he perched himself at the back.

Then came the part of the service where a few were asked to give testimonies about their spiritual journey. Susan could not believe her eyes when Fareed walked onto the stage. Yes, it was him. She remembered from the lab room. She rubbed her eyes as if to clear invisible cobwebs.

"I am from Iraq, and I am sure most of you have heard about our country. I grew up as a Muslim in downtown Baghdad at the height of the war, Fareed went on. As he continued recounting his story including his relationship with Jesus, Susan could not hold back tears running down her cheeks. *Was this happening,* she thought. And as he was about to finish, Fareed made a very fundamental statement. I love my Muslim brothers and sisters, but I have now found a faith in Jesus. It is my desire to walk with him and to make him known. Thank you."

As he came down from the pulpit, people were clapping, beating drums. The atmosphere was electric. Here was a young man at university from Iraq who seemed to have found his purpose on planet earth. Auntie Grace stared at Susan smiling as if sending an encrypted message!

By the time the youth leader preached, the environment was conducive for receiving the message. It was one of the best services so far since Susan became one of the church members.

Pastor Stanley looked very satisfied and hopeful for the future life of his church.

"Aren't you going to congratulate the other young people for doing so well? Auntie Grace asked Susan. Especially that young man from Iraq with such a magnificent testimony", She smiled at Susan as if to making a hint.

Susan looked a bit shy. "Alright auntie, I will have to wait until there is an opportunity to do so. There are still many people trying to do the same." She started pushing Auntie Grace in her wheelchair towards the entrance. A few students had already started congratulating those who had given testimonies including Fareed. Many of the girls had different agendas and motives.

"Thank you, guys, that was really good", Susan started her congratulatory handshakes, until she got to Fareed. "Hey that was good. Didn't I see you in the lab the other day?" Susan quickly moved on to shake the other girls who had given testimonies. She did not give Fareed time to answer. In any case he was overwhelmed by the response so far. But he noted Susan's comments.

The topic for discussion during the drive back to Auntie Grace's house was predictable. The service was extraordinary. And for Auntie Grace, it was Fareed's testimony that overshadowed all the others.

"Girls, you still have a life to live. I don't know whether you saw what I saw. All those young people were very good, but that boy from Iraq, he is special, Auntie Grace quipped. Open your eyes girls. Sorry close your eyes often. I mean you must pray seriously and ask God to lead you." she went on. Susan was aware what Auntie Grace was alluding to. She wished she did not let the cat out of the bag. This was her assignment. Susan was convinced that there was something here. She did not want to push things but to wait, as her mother used to tell here. She kept everything in her heart.

Fareed became something of a celebrity, following his testimony at the church. His was a fascinating story not only because of his encounter with Jesus as a Muslim, but because of the war in Iraq which was still raging. Just the mention of him being from Iraq, brought mixed emotions from a segment of the student population the majority of whom were Americans. For those who were in the church that day, their attitude towards Fareed was somehow tinted. Yes, they believed what he said about Jesus, but he remained an Iraqi. *Was he still a Muslim or his testimony was merely a cover up? Was he different from the Iraqis that the media had portrayed? Was he not part of those that the US army was fighting against who were remnants of the old regime?* No one could answer these questions, except Fareed. This meant that from then on, many would watch Fareed's movements closely in and out of campus.

Not so with Susan. The night of the Youth Service, she had so much to share with her roommate even though they did not quite share the same faith. Josephine had nothing against God as she would say, and yet she did not fancy the idea of a full blown, head over heels love for religion.

"Jos Susan shouted from the kitchen where she was trying to rescue overcooked morsels.

"What is it now, how was church. You haven't said a word since you came back," Josephine responded.

"Hold on, love. I will just finish frying these poor morsels, and I will tell you. It was fab, exhilarating, ridiculously great. Wicked almost," Susan could not hold her excitement. This was the first time Susan really showed joy and excitement since she moved to share a flat with Josephine.

Susan did not want to bore Josephine with details concerning their drive through auntie Grace's house.

Susan continued, "I have never felt so emotional in a church service before. And strange, our pastor was nowhere to be seen. He tucked himself at the back of the church and let the guys and gals take over. But … I don't know whether I should share this with you. Do you know a guy called Fareed? She asked.

Josephine: "You mean Fareed Hassan? Jos replied. He is in my year. He is cool I must say, I mean cool. I had a crush on him the first time I saw him, Josephine went on. Sorry Susan I didn't mean to steal the thunder out of your story. Go on what happened? Is he your boyfriend?"

Josephine was a loudmouth sometimes. But this time she could not help it because Fareed was quite a character and she meant it when she said she had a crush on him.

Susan: "Thanks Jos."

Susan went on to explain what happened including Fareed's testimony, her encounter in the library and how impressed she was with him. Although she did not know him, she thought highly of him. Susan was careful not to mention her sentiments towards Fareed. She felt it better to keep this to herself.

Josephine: "Seriously Susan, is he someone you could consider dating? Don't get me wrong, I am not saying this is something you are thinking about".

Susan: "That's ok Jos. You know I am big girl now and these are issues that I grapple with from time to time. Unlike you, I have a difficult mountain to climb. Let's face it, I am black from Zimbabwe and studying in the USA. Do you get what I am saying? It's not easy love. So, when you see descent guys like Fareed pop up from nowhere you begin to ask yourself questions. Is it fate, is it coincidence or for someone like me who believes that my life is led and controlled by God, is it God bringing someone to my attention? I get confused sometimes and wonder who will marry me, if ever that is going to happen. Anyway, that was what happened at the church service. I hope you will be able to join us someday Jos."

Jos could not make out what this meant. *Could this be the beginning of something big? If only Susan could free herself from this race chip on her shoulder attitude and grab what comes as quickly as possible. Not so easy she thought. Easier said than done. These are real issues, Culture, Prejudice, Racism. This is the world we are living in, and navigating these, needs a lot of wisdom, patience, and character.*

CHAPTER 11
LOVE HURTS

Following her eyeball-to-eyeball restaurant experience with Keith, it was never business as usual for Mel as their relationship began to intensify. They met frequently and were on the phone myriads of times. Keith decided not to open to his friends about his relationship. He wanted to tread very carefully in case something went wrong like his former relationship. He believed that this time God was going to honour his promise and allow them to marry. He dreamed of a big wedding, probably at the cathedral. If not at a prestigious hall. His dad had the resources and of course his son's marriage would mean the world to him. He imagined this as a celebration and a time to bring friends and family across the globe, not to mention his colleagues in the corporate world.

Keith rarely went home because of the nature of his work. His normal day as a solicitor involved examining different cases and submissions to court. Their firm was one of the busiest in town and they hardly had time to relax. This weekend he was able to mix business with pleasure. His client was based just a few miles from his hometown. He took this opportunity to visit dad.

"What a surprise", dad quipped as Keith walked through the door. They hugged and immediately sat comfortably side by side. There was so much to talk about including reminiscing over dad's birthday a few months before. Brine was glad that this subject had been brought up as he had a few questions to ask Keith.

"You didn't quite tell me who that girl was. I mean is she just a friend or something serious. You know we have not talked about this since.," Brine went on. Keith knew that this was serious, and dad really wanted to know.

Keith: "Sorry dad, I thought when auntie asked the same question, you understood my answer, Keith spoke softly to his dad. There was no turning back. He would have to make it official to his dad.

Keith: She is my girlfriend dad, and I am planning to marry her. I am really in love with her. She is a good Christian girl and I believe that she has been the one that I have been waiting for."

Brine: "Keith, I am glad that you are serious about this relationship. You will forgive me for being cautious as your father. I have been through this before and last time unfortunately God decided to take your friend away. I still hurt at times. She was a very committed Christian and we were all excited about it. And she was from Oxford, English through and through. We had no misgivings, and we were comfortable," Brine spoke slowly.

Keith: "But ... dad, Keith interjected, That was yesterday. And if you are worried about Mel's colour or race, please let me know. I know I have never experienced such a relationship, but dad, I love Melissa. I may not be able to anticipate all the challenges that we might face because of this decision, but all I know is that she fits the bill. She is committed to me and so am I. Yes, I have been hurt before but I can't stop now with God on my side. You know dad, this is the time that I wish mum was alive. I would do with a shoulder to cry on", Keith started to cry.

Brine: "Keith, please don't go that route. I too have been on that journey. Do you think I don't wish if your mum was here? All these years looking after you and your sister? Son, love hurts. Sometimes I feel so alone in this house which over the years has become emptier and emptier since your mum died and you and your sister left." *Brine had not anticipated such a serious discussion earlier on in Keith's relationship with Melissa, let alone before meeting and knowing Melissa. He felt rather sad that this had happened, and yet he thought of no appropriate time than this to take the bull by its horns. This was an opportunity to alert his son of some of the issues he had to consider earlier on in his relationship.* They spoke at length and decided that it was imperative for dad to meet Melissa one of the days. Brine was keen to do so, and they had their own truce for now until a later time.

Melissa's excitement over her newly found boyfriend had become infectious. While she kept this as a secret to let things mature a little, she could not hold this to her chest any longer. Understandably, there was a certain visible vibrancy and emotional umph in Melissa's appearance wherever she went, whether in dealing with her legal clients or generally in the way she responded to people. One of her colleagues even remarked on how Melissa's work desk had now been transformed into a Vision Board with colourful mementos conspicuously arranged. She did not stay home anymore but would visit mum and dad from time to time. And each time she went home, she always wanted to slip into her old bean bag like the good old times. She always remembered that it was from that bean bag that she had asked her mum and dad the infamous question, "Who will marry me?" How time had quickly passed by since that day. Still, she was glad that she had the guts then to be inquisitive.

On one beautiful summer afternoon she decided to visit her parents. She wasn't sure how the encounter would pan out. How would his dad respond to the news that at last she believed that God had graciously provided someone who would be a friend for life. And this time not someone from the sticks of Zimbabwe but from Oxford of all places!

She parked the car in their driveway and sneaked through the back door.

"Mum, dad, I am home", Mel shouted expecting a sudden flurry of ululation from her mother as was their custom.

There was an eerie silence for a moment and in unison, mum and dad burst into a praise song as they slowly walked downstairs. This was strange, as dad rarely sang in tune. *Were they privy to information about her new boyfriend*? she thought. *Did they have good news to share with her.* They hugged and hugged. Melissa went straight to her old bean bag. This was the platform from where she would make her announcement!

There was so much to talk about. She told them about her work and how her firm continued to serve many clients both local and international. The number of immigration cases meant that a good number of people were being deported.

Mum: "How are you Melissa, I mean your life, has anything changed? -Mum spoke in her soft almost inaudible voice- Your dad and I sometimes worry about ... whether ... you know what I mean. She had started clawing into the rough terrain of Mel's life. And of course, Mel knew where this was going.

Melissa: "Mum, dad, I have good news for you. *Melissa paused as she realised that culturally she should not tell her parents point blank about her relationship. This was the preserve of the aunties and uncles in the village back home. But there were no unties and uncles. In any case, she thought, I was able to ask them about who will marry me, why can't I break the good news to them first.*

Melissa: Mum and dad, I really have good news. I have found a friend whom I believe would like to marry me, she smiled as she focussed her eyes on mum and dad, clearly wanting to see their initial reaction.

Dad: "Where is he from, I mean is he black, from Zimbabwe. How did you know him", dad asked the typical questions with cultural overtones?

Mum: "Melissa, Oh Lord, isn't this an answer to prayer. Is he a Christian? Are you sure he is the one? Tell us a little about him, *mum responded in her typical Christocentric manner.* I appreciate it but I want to know more." Thoughts started flooding her mind. *Visions of a son in law for her first born. She reflected on years of praying for her sibling amid negative insinuations from relations and some from the church, let alone her sisters who now had grandchildren. This was a new dawn for her. It meant the world to her, and she couldn't wait to hear from Melissa who this character was and how she had met him.*

Melissa: "Mum and dad, he is English and comes from Oxford. But the important thing is that I really love him, and I believe that God brought us together in a special way at this time", Melissa finally responded. There was an eerie silence, rather spooky. Dad especially, could not hide his discomfort. *Had he heard right that her daughter's boyfriend was an Englishman? And from Oxford? Reality had now set in. What they hoped and prayed for had now been realised in a way they did not expect.*

It took some time for TK to process what he had just heard. *Here was his loving daughter, for years on "the market" as it were, now announcing that she had found the love of her life. His imagination ran riot. He thought of the village in rural Zimbabwe where he was raised, the rules of engagement concerning marriage, the norms, the cultural etiquette. And here he was thousands of miles away listening to his daughter talking about an English boyfriend.* The excitement and enthusiasm with which Melissa broke the news caught TK off guard. It was clear that that there was little room for negotiation. His daughter had made up her mind. Period. He however, thought he would still try and bring sanity to the whole situation. And yet on the other hand, he knew that this, in a way, was the consequence of their decision to relocate. A matter of their decisions impacting on their daughter's destiny".

There was clearly a flurry of activity in TK's brain. All these thoughts were flooding in, and it was clear that he and his wife would need to continue to talk about this long after their daughter had left.

Mum: "You haven't told us much about your friend. Is he English or maybe he was just born here, and his parents come from Africa or Jamaica? Or perhaps he is an African American", Melissa's mother slowly prodded further hoping for an acceptable answer.

Melissa: "Sorry, Keith is an Englishman from the heart of Oxford. You know Oxford. I am sure you have heard of the reputable Oxford university, one of the best universities in the world. His mother passed away years ago after a long illness. His sister still lives near Oxford with her husband. They have one child. His relatives are dotted all over the world including Australia, where his auntie lives."

It was clear now that what Melissa's parents feared had just happened. They were not prepared for this. They thought of their friends and the many conversations they had had in the past about this. Sometimes taking part in ridiculing those families whose children had succumbed to the pressure and married in the Diaspora. They now realised the enormity of the task. *How would they navigate these stormy cultural waters? What mattered most was that Melissa had found a friend. Her prayer was now answered and what was left was to pray that the relationship comes to its logical conclusion. Marriage, the wedding were now up for grabs. All these things kept flooding the minds of TK and his wife.*

Dad: "Why Keith? Were you not able to go for someone closer home, I mean …?

Melissa: "A black guy, dad. Is that what you are talking

about? Never mind, I thought I would tell you because I know you have been concerned about me and what was going to happen to my life. It is always difficult to comprehend God's ways. I never thought that all along God was on my case concerning whom to marry. Please continue to pray for me so that …" Melissa started to cry. She was overwhelmed. Here she was at home with the best news in her life and somehow, her parents seemed like nit-picking on her decision. *It was unfair,* she thought. *However, deep down she realised that while her parents were putting on a negative stance, they too were happy for her. It will only be a matter of time before their joy burst at the seams.*

Dad: "Melissa, Melissa, it's just too much of a shock for us. We have nothing against what you have done but…"

Dad responded as he came over to the bean bag. He held her hand. Mum slipped into the bean bag to embrace Melissa. She started sobbing uncontrollably too. She was sixty-one. She had become the talk of the neighbourhood among Zimbabweans. Most of them had grandchildren and were wondering whether it would ever be possible for Melissa to get married. Here she was witnessing the beginning of her daughter's relationship. How it would pan out was not her business, but she was happy her daughter was "normal". She could fall in love and God had done it for her.

It took some time before they all recovered. Melissa quickly made cups of tea for all of them. This was an emotional afternoon for mum and dad. Melissa showed them one of Keith's photos with his dad at his dad's birthday. She mentioned that he too was a solicitor like her and was doing very well. She spoke of his commitment to Jesus Christ and how active he was in the church, even though he had gone through difficult times in the past. His former girlfriend had died tragically before they could get married. However, he had now recovered from that and was so in love with Melissa that he prayed that this time all would go well. By the time they finished drinking tea, they all seemed relieved and more relaxed. They had gone through the first hurdle, but more work remained. There were practical issues to tackle; the attitudes, the mindset, naysayers, the cultural hurdles. But they had a feeling that after this encounter they were on the same page. Come wind come weather they all wanted this relationship to work.

Keith had already been embraced as part of the family. It was almost ten past ten when Melissa said goodbye. She had a court case to attend to the following day.

Melissa: "Mum, Dad thank you very much for listening to me. I am so happy that we were able to talk about this," she went on.

Dad: "I must admit, it has not been easy, but I am happy for you, my daughter. Please let us know how you get along. Don't hesitate to stop this relationship must you feel it is no longer working," her dad slowly began to advise her as Melissa walked out of the house, with her mum clutching to her daughter. She quickly hugged her daughter as she rushed to her car before driving off into the night.

CHAPTER 12
CHANGE IN THE AIR

Jade had just come back from the pub after a long day at work. She looked knackered and remained tucked into the tiny chair in her upstairs bedsit. Thanks to the local council, she was able to get accommodation because of her two-year old sibling. Every day she had to juggle between work, nursery school and household chores. Sometimes she felt abandoned and had on many occasions contemplated suicide. She started flipping through the channels and stopped when she saw what looked like a boat full of migrants floating in the sea. The reporter had just started. *And here we see migrants from many countries who are stranded on a rubber dinghy. It is reported that until the Red Cross Ship found them, they were in danger of capsizing. Many lives have been lost these few months. Children, young men, and women and in one instance a twenty-year-old pregnant girl. It's awful. One cannot imagine that this is happening in the 21st century.* Jade was stunned tears rolling down her red cheeks. She looked at her daughter sleeping on the couch, a reminder of her dad whom Jade had met at the local gym. He was tall dark and cutely cut from the best Africa could produce. It was not long after Jade was pregnant that he just walked away, and she never saw him again. Jade, while bitter about her friend still had sympathy for these migrants who were part of her daughters DNA. She could not run away from the fact that she too was in a way part of the broader African family. She carried part of Africa and the immigrant community in her loins for nine months! She thought, *Who knows, in that boat could be my daughter Maddie's relation, may be a cousin. Perhaps among all the immigrants coming to Europe could be someone very close to Hassim, the boyfriend who dumped her." And from watching a clip of the television news, a flood of thoughts reigned in and left her confused. What is happening to this world, she thought? Why can't the world act as one and embrace others as human beings?* She knew this was wishful thinking. The real world was somehow tearing itself apart.

Jade's story was replicated across the community. With many coming from different parts of the world to live in this Borough, people were getting used to the new dispensation. While in the past people from different countries were dotted and far between, it was now clear that things had changed. In pubs, libraries, schools, there was evidence of a diverse community. The response to this situation varied from place to place and from person to person. Some embraced it as the new norm and yet others negatively looked at it as the new normal which meant they had to get used to it before they could embrace it. Programmes had been put in place to try and bring diverse communities together. Programmes on Foster Care ensured that families could take care of needy migrants and others who were in dire straits. The hope was that some form of integration would take place and ensure that communities lived together in peace and harmony. This is the community that Melissa, George, Charlotte lived. This was overwhelming for Jade. For now, all she could think of was her daughter, and how she was going to make ends meet. The thought of Hassim suddenly appearing from oblivion was a nonstarter. *She often thought of her friends from school who seemed to be better off. Would she be settled one day? A proper husband, family. Her imagination ran riot. Perhaps she would be married someday. In church? She thought, "Who would really want to marry me after all that had happened to me." No sane bloke would ever want to get involved with a Carer with a black daughter. She continued to get more and more depressed the more she thought of her present predicament.*

Maddie started wriggling from the couch where she was sleeping. Jade knew that it was time to get her to bed. And very soon she would have to go to bed too as she was starting early the following day.

While the school Jade went was a few miles from Melissa's, they often met on the bus and were in talking terms. Jade had always admired Mel for the way she seemed to carry herself. She was courteous always smiling, and respectful to the elderly. Jade guessed that this may be because of Melisa's upbringing in an African household. She gave up imitating her. Hers was a household of real raw English people. There was a lot of swearing and aggression in the home. She had witnessed dad shouting at mum a few times. He had very little time with the children. Jade for some reason, had respect for the likes of Melissa and somehow grew up respecting and appreciating members of the community who were not necessarily English by birth. And when she bumped into Tino, she had a crush on him. He came across as a fatherly figure who listened a lot and very caring. He was different from what Jade was experiencing at home. And whenever they met, Jade felt safe and assured. She had found someone who really appreciated him.

Tino was staying with his mother at the time in a small flat, while they waited for proper accommodation from the Council. Jade would occasionally sneak into Tino's flat when his mum was away at work.

On one occasion, just as Jade was making herself comfortable on the sofa, with Tino in the kitchen, mum walked in. She was supposed to be working all day, but her shift had been cancelled without her knowing.

"Is it you Tino in the kitchen? They have cancelled my shift again. Unbelievable."

Jade froze in the sofa, while Tino rushed to meet mum in the foyer.

Tino: "Hi mum, can you help me fix something in the kitchen", Tino tried to divert mum from going for the small lounge where Jade was. She headed straight to the lounge without responding to Tino.

Mum: "Hello, who are you, what are you doing in my house? she blurted as she came face to face with Jade. Listen you, I don't care who you are, don't come into my house to ruin my boy. We don't do those things here. Does your mum know you are here?"

Tino's mum spoke out. Tino came quickly to escort Jade to

the door. He knew what her mother thought about bringing girlfriends into the house unless they had been properly introduced to the family. Tino knew the rules, but he was also under pressure. This was a shocker for Jade. She was not welcome unless a miracle happened. This was an experience of a lifetime.

The sudden burst of anger and rage from Tino's mother Gloria was unexpected and yet understandable. It was like she was reliving her past in the village forty-five years ago. She came from a normal but strict upbringing which was in line with their culture. You see, it was taboo for any child however old they were to bring in friends of the opposite sex unannounced. You either gave notice of your intention as a child or you kept your friendship outside the home. Many children lived in fear because everyone in the village was a bona fide mum and dad, who could "spy" on you. You had to have readymade answers in case you were caught by a neighbour with a friend they were not sure of. It was their responsibility to inform your parents of your tomfoolery as they regarded it. It was not until your relationship was known officially that you could walk about with glee. Gloria knew all this and even when she grew up and went to boarding school, the cultural shadow seemed to follow her. Sometimes it felt like one was under surveillance all the time. It had its advantages but sometimes parents overdid it without calmly explaining to their children the value of this cultural norm. Gloria's generation failed to ward off the stigma attached to this kind of behaviour. You could hardly discuss your concerns about relationships with your parents. You were either in it for the long haul or you were not. And for those fortunate to go to Boarding schools, it was a celebration of their newfound freedom. There were no holds barred for many and what was taboo in the village became the new normal with its consequences.

Gloria's response to Jade was uncharacteristic for a lady well known in church circles. She had been in the UK for several years and this was the first time she let go of her temper. The rest of the day, she struggled to get back her composure as she reflected on what had just happened. The past seemed to have overtaken the present. In a moment of rage, she had made a very poignant statement concerning her boy's relationships let alone Jade's regard for her. The message was loud and clear. She may now have been living in a new environment, away from her village, but the old rules still applied. There was no compromise. Either you stick to my rules within my house as my parents used to or you don't. The fact that her son had invited Jade was neither here nor there. Jade should have known of herself that she was giving in to something that was just not done in that neighbourhood. By the time Tino came back from escorting Jade, it was late in the evening.

Mum: "So, who was that girl Tino?", his mum slowly asked, with a grin on her face.

She realised that this was going to be an uphill battle to unravel this very complicated episode and help make sense of it. While Tino had great respect for his mother, he was rather surprised that mum was this serious and aggressive. This was a part of mum that he really did not know. Gloria had left Zimbabwe when Tino was eight years old. She came on a visitor's Visa and never went back because she did not have the necessary papers. She went underground until she was able to apply for asylum. This took her another five years for her to be considered a bona fide resident. This was when she was able to bring her only son. Tino was now sixteen. Since then, Gloria was careful to treat Tino with kid gloves as she continued to appreciate her son after many years of separation. And it seemed like some cultural values had been put in the back burner in her house. Tino too had enjoyed the best of both worlds. While he was "home," he lived with his grandparents, who treated him like a king. They considered him like an orphan since his mother was away and could not come to see him. And meanwhile mum would send loads of cash and goodies which made him live like a mini king. For Tino, coming to join his mother was a continuation of the good life that he enjoyed at home. There were no cultural issues to worry about. Besides, this was the UK and freedom was in the air.

Tino: "Her name is Jade, We go to college together. She lives not far from here.

Mum: "Tino, We have never talked about life, have we? I mean how you as an African boy are expected to behave. I know that I did not have this opportunity because you grew up at home. I am hoping that we will have such a discussion. This is to safeguard you from this community here. You are African and you should not forget that. I am sure there are many African girls at the college. Some of these white girls are a bit dodgy because they were not taught properly."

Tino's mum Gloria slowly began her road to rebooting her relationship with her son. It was an uphill struggle as she realised that she had already messed up big time when she lost control of her feelings. She hoped and prayed that Tino would forgive and forget and begin to listen to his mother's advice and reasons why she had blurted out against Jade.

Tino: "Mum, I am not ready to talk about this now. Can we discuss this tomorrow? I need time to process this," Tino responded. This was a loaded answer for Gloria. *My son wants to process what I have said and done?",* she thought. Suddenly, Gloria realised what had happened and who he was dealing with. This was not the kid she left home many years ago, but someone who seemed to have matured and who was able to consider things before responding to them. This was scary. For once Gloria felt like a child inside as she saw maturity in her only son.

Jade was devastated after being chucked out of Tino's house. Here she was trying to make up for a lost life. She looked at her only daughter, a product of a messy relationship that saw her being treated like a piece of meat by her other boyfriend.

In fact, when Jade started dating James, it all looked promising. James's mother was a professional woman, organised and very close to her three siblings. She was a widow and long forgotten about her husband who died in tragic circumstances on the motorway. His car had broken down and while he was still in the car phoning the Breakdown company, he was hit from behind by a lorry which had veered off the hard shoulder. Apparently, the driver lost control of the vehicle due to a momentary loss of concentration because he was tired. He had driven hundreds of miles in the week and the body gave in. By the time the paramedics arrived he had lost a lot of blood. Still the air ambulance quickly flew him to the nearest hospital where he was pronounced dead on arrival.

James's mum was left devastated, and it took her years to recover, although memories of her beloved husband still lingered on. She had made it a point not to concentrate on the past, but to exert all her energy into making sure her three children got all the support they needed. She was a good Christian woman who worked hard to instil Christian values in her children. She had come to the United kingdom on a proper working visa and because all her children were under eighteen, they came on her visa too. They went to the best schools in the neighbourhood. This is where James met Jade.

It started one afternoon while boarding the bus from school. James tried to jump the queue and Jade snapped.

Jade: "Excuse me, we all want to get home you know. Please can you come back behind the queue." James was always trying to wind girls up as some form of entertainment. Sometimes he got away with it and sometimes he didn't. In fact, back in his village school he was once punished for doing the same thing when he kept cracking jokes to a group of girls who were doing serious homework. Jade won and James sheepishly went to the back of the queue.

"Thanks Jade. That was brave. He is a nutter sometimes," some of the girls giggled in response. On the bus, James was keen to try his luck again with Jade. He porched himself next to her and sat silent, trying to provoke Jade.

Jade: "Why did you do that", Jade broke the silence

"You are mean you are", James answered back.

"What's your name?

"'I am James. I am in 4 S, Mr Nichol's class.

"Are you the boy who is always in detention. My friend Ivonne is in your class, and she has talked about the likes of you". Jade started to unravel a bit of James's baggage.

James: "Shush, what has that to do with me sitting here. Can we talk about something else?", James quickly killed the subject. By the time Jade got off the bus, they had built up some sort of understanding of each other.

James continued to meet with Jade many times after the bus incident. At the shops, for a Costa coffee and at one time they went to the movies together. Jade began to appreciate James's sense of humour and each time they met, Jade was left screaming with laughter. It was fun. After their O levels they went to the same local College and were doing Arts. They met more frequently and begun talking about their options after they left College. Jade was keen to go to University, while James wanted to go into teaching. It was clear that this relationship was becoming closer and closer and very soon they would need to redefine it.

It was as they were watching the film Mama Mia that something started to kick in. Was it love or mere infatuation?

While they enjoyed the film, they left the theatre having thoughts in their heads; unspoken but conspicuous. *Was this the beginning of a deeper relationship?* James thought *or was this a red flag to warn him to slow down.* This went on for a while and because they did not talk about it, they bulldozed their way until Jade succumbed. The next thing Jade phoned James.

Jade: James where are you. I want to talk to you?" He had just finished his exam on Critical thinking.

James: "Hey Jade, you sound serious. What do you want to talk about? Let's meet up tomorrow at McDonald's. My exam today was tough. I am not sure if I made sense.

Jade: "No James. Let's meet today. I am at the Bus station in town. Let's meet for a few minutes. There is something I want to tell you." She sounded serious, and James complied. He could see from where he was as he approached her that there was something serious.

James: "What's up?"

Jade: "I had a pregnant test".

James froze for a second. It hit him like a ton of bricks.

James: "So, I mean why a pregnancy test".

Jade: "What do you mean why? You have made me pregnant James. I am seventeen. Do you know what that means?"

It was difficult to hold a sane conversation with all the adrenaline flowing through both, especially James. Here he was, talking about a pregnancy and possible fatherhood when he was just finishing his A Levels. What would befall him when his mother got wind of this knowing what she had gone through as a widow. Not to mention his late dad, who, wherever he is out there would still find this unacceptable.

James: "Jade is that all you wanted to tell me. Are you sure it is from me; I mean the pregnancy? How do I know.", James spoke like a typical male chauvinist, not willing to take responsibility? It was difficult to see where he got this from. He was only eighteen and had grown up in the UK for the best part of his life. It looked like this attitude was not limited to one culture but seemed to be all over the globe wherever men existed.

The two had stood at the bus stop for nearly two hours punctuated by a deathly silence. Reality began to set in. Both would still complete their studies but for Jade she would have to have her baby first before she thought of her next moves. University was out for the following year. For now, the big hurdle was letting their parents know of what had happened. James was from Zambia and Jade's parents came from the northeast of England.

Both Jade and James were not prepared for what was about to unravel. This always came as a shock to parents throughout the community. While issues of equality and oneness were always espoused in the media, in churches and other fora, the reality was never fully discussed to help young men and women cope. And because of the immigrant situation in the country as well as Europe and the Americas, there was need to tackle these issues not only economically but relationally. What was to be young peoples' response to this. Who were they to associate with and to what extent? Was it fine to seek deeper relationships in a sometimes-hostile environment? Who would marry a young person whom some communities were not comfortable with? Was it possible to find someone to marry given all the challenges of intercultural, interracial marriages? Where would one get advice to be able to make an informed choice about this. Or was it now better not to think about it.

The parents too were in a similar dilemma. Many in the community were brought up to think differently and what was happening was a new normal for them. The world of Jade and James was becoming complicated. They needed to reconfigure their beliefs in a world they had never experienced but which demanded their response if they were to survive.

CHAPTER 13
LOVE WITH NO LIMITS

Following Fareed's testimony at the youth Service and the positive responses he received especially from Susan, Josephine Susan's roommate was keen to connect these two. She had given up dreaming about Fareed as she felt she was not up to scratch. *Susan and Fareed were the real deal,* Josephine thought. And when she bumped into him after the auditorium lecture, she was keen to use the opportunity to explore further the possibilities.

Josephine: "Fareed, I heard that you were at church the other day and that many people seemed to like your testimony. I didn't know you were serious about religion." Josephine went on.

Fareed: "Jos, who told you. Since when were you interested in church things. Yes, I was told it went well. I am glad I was able to share what I believe. It means a lot to me.," he smiled at Josephine.

Josephine: "Susan told me. You don't know her, but she says she met you in the lab the other day. She is such a nice girl. She is my roommate. She is from Zimbabwe. Do you remember her." Jos further probed Fareed.

Fareed: "Oh yes I remember her. Was she at church? I don't quite remember, thanks for telling me", Fareed walked the steps to his next lecture while Jos disappeared into the College restaurant to grab a burger.

Things had begun to change in the USA. There were news reports of shootings within College campuses and while these were not attributed to terrorism, it was still scary. Politically so much careless talk was broadcast in the media regarding immigrants. The land of opportunity was beginning to earn a not so grand reputation. While this did not affect Susan's College, many were fearful of the spill over from other States. Fareed had always been careful from the day he arrived in the country. His country of birth did not help things either and the aftermath of the war brought in difficulties especially for the young people who were mostly held in suspicion the moment they set foot on American soil. Fareed was no exception.

His greatest hope was that after his Chemical Engineering studies he would be able to land a lucrative job in America or some of the more progressive countries in the West. For now, going back to Iraq was not plausible because of the security situation. Besides, her family had now moved to Qatar following the end of his dad's diplomatic career and the resumption of his engineering career. However, Fareed decided to concentrate on his studies.

Susan was doubly surprised when he took his place by the corner in the lab to find Fareed again in the lab. He seemed busy with his experiments with a group of other students who were milling around him. He seemed to be the one doing the demonstrations and everyone else watching. Susan and the other girls started doing their experiments as well and for two hours they were all at it, problem solving. It was a relief when it was over, and fortunately, Susan did not have a class after that. Fareed caught Susan's eye and came straight to where she was busy packing her things.

Fareed: "Hello, Josephine told me you are her roommate. Honestly, I had not remembered that you were at the Youth service the other Sunday. What have you done to Jos.? She now seems to have an interest in church issues." Fareed went on trying to break the ice and seeking to get a response from Susan: "Oh, hello Fareed, or dare I say Mr preacher man. I must say I was very impressed by your talk," *Susan continued to walk towards the door. Some girls were now too close for comfort, and she wanted some space. And besides, this was an opportunity to get to know this gentleman from nowhere.*

Fareed: "It's not easy to stand before such a large crowd and try and make sense of anything."

Susan: "I think you did very well. What is it like in Iraq? It must be different from our Zimbabwe where I come from. But your president was very popular in our country before he died." Susan began rumbling in the hope that this could be the introduction to something, who knows what. She was hoping from the time she met Fareed that God's will would be done regarding who she was going to find as a partner in her life.

For a first-time encounter, the conversation went beyond

expectation. And by the time they parted, it was clear that something of essence was beginning to materialise.

"Catch you later," Fareed shouted as he ran upstairs.

Susan just looked towards Fareed in awe that she had broken the ice. The boy she met in the lab was now featuring in her life. At least for now. How long, she could not tell. She was pleased that at least he had become a subject of her conversation and that of Jos. How things change, she thought. The lab, the church, auntie Grace and now the personal encounter. In her spirit, she began to praise God for this thing which was about to explode into something hopefully designed by God from the very beginning. *Dream on Susan,* she thought. *And as Auntie Grace had said before, she would have to close her eyes, meaning she had work to do on her knees.*

Fareed had very few friends, mostly from his year group. The majority were from the USA and a few from the Middle East especially Qatar and the United Arab Emirates. His mother had grown up in the Gulf region where her father worked for Gulf Oil, one of the biggest Oil conglomerates in the region. She spoke very fluent Arabic even though she was born in Cincinnati. Her connection with the United States endeared her very well to Americans during the war in Iraq. It was a safety net as she could get away with it when there was animosity between the USA and Iraq. And for Fareed, it was easier to associate with lads from the region because of his father. The only problem he found was that a few of these friends embraced his new love for Jesus, whom they only

Who will marry me?

regarded as one of the prophets and nothing more. However, this did not prevent them from talking about those things that they had in common. The only exception was Raji Musa, who for some reason had, like Fareed turned a page in his relationship with God. He was one of the young people at the Youth service where Fareed made a mark following his testimony about his relationship with Jesus. These two were always in conversation with one another, sharing their struggles and working out how to reconfigure their faith among some dudes who were not in sync with religion.

Fareed was very keen to share his encounter with Susan. Although he did not know her that well, there was something about her which he could not figure out. Before he came to the United States, he had never met a black girl let alone an African girl who came from Zimbabwe. He was a bit embarrassed that he could not even place Zimbabwe on the map. He had vaguely heard about a "dictator" from Zimbabwe, just like Susan had heard about a "dictator" from Iraq. The man who had ruled that country for decades. Here he was now on campus, having a conversation with a girl from that country. Susan was no ordinary girl. Beauty was a given, but she was very purposeful and honest. She did not shy away from speaking her mind. Such clarity was a preserve of the wise from another planet. *And here she was, Fareed thought, in his path, available and willing to share her thoughts.* Since becoming a Christian, Fareed had been taught the importance of waiting upon God. That one had to be clear about what God wanted in one's life and the importance of making a good and informed decision. As he grew older especially during his second year at University, it became imperative. The urge to love somebody was becoming more and more forceful. And with the many students he saw pairing on campus, "desperation" was beginning to raise her ugly head.

Fareed: "Hey Raji," do you ever think of being married one day?" Fareed, unexpectedly sprung this stinger on Raji.

Raji: "Hey, where is that coming from. We are still on campus, remember? You still haven't completed your Chemical engineering degree. Why talk of marriage when you don't even have a girlfriend. At least one that I know of. Unless something has happened in the last twenty-four hours." Raji tried to avoid answering the question

Raji, equally surprising Fareed by his long winded but insightful answer which showed a level of maturity that Fareed did not think Raji had.

Fareed: "Come on Raji, it is just a question. Some thoughts wondering in my head. Sometimes it is good to plan and be proactive. You don't want these things to happen suddenly and catch you unprepared. At least we can think about this. But to be quite honest, in the last two weeks something has happened which has suddenly made me realise that I need to think and pray about this and not to wait until the nick of time, Fareed seemed fired up to share. You see, for some reason I have been meeting this girl, you know her, she is Jos's roommate, and she comes from Zimbabwe"

Raji: "That is in Africa isn't it", retorted Raji. You are beginning to worry me, Fareed. Do you know where Africa is.

Have you been there before, let alone think of someone from there? Let me give you a bit of history I got from my dad. Parts of East Africa were colonised by Arabs who came to trade in spices and herbs

Fareed: "Raji, I am not talking about history here. I am saying there is this fine Christian girl, whom I have been in contact with who has really triggered my thoughts regarding the future. She may not be the one I am going to marry, but her footprints on campus have made me admire who she is and what such a person could mean to anyone contemplating marriage. To be quite honest, I love her. I have not told her but somehow it seems what is happening is a clear indicator of where we are both headed even though she still does not know my feelings about her."

Fareed was beginning to talk like someone who had an apparition of some sort. He spoke with clarity and conviction. And the fact that Susan was from Africa was neither here nor there. All he was looking for was what God had intended for him. The criteria had to do with her relationship with God and not based on culture, ethnicity, or anything else. You could see spiritual maturity coming through from Fareed. At least he had shared with his friend and really made known his position regarding what sort of person he would eventually marry. It was clear that the two would continue this conversation for some time. Raji was keen to meet this girl that Fareed seemed to adore and revere.

Raji: "Alright, "Raji raised his hands as if to surrender. The proof of the pudding is in the eating. I am looking forward to meeting your Susan, even though she is not really yours yet!

There was no doubt that Fareed was tilting towards Susan. In his mind he could not justify such attachment to a girl who was culturally so different from him. Surprisingly, that was not the issue now. He sensed a certain attraction towards her. She was beautiful alright, but she was smart too. She was not like the ordinary African woman he had read about in magazines. She seemed to speak her mind and her conviction to her faith was something Fareed admired. She wasn't the loose woman type. It was one thing to admire her traits, it was another to translate this into real love action. How would he break the ice? And as he thought about this, he wondered how this could go down with his parents and his uncle back in Basra who seemed to breathe racist fire each time he saw people from other countries. His uncle would prefer a white woman to a black girl. For some reason, his love for Arab traders in Africa meant that he always looked down upon black people as outcasts and fit only to be slaves. His was an obsolete view of the world but a very infectious one. There was no doubt that Fareed was in a dilemma; either to please his parents and relations or to follow his heart based on his conviction in a God who answers prayer.

It was late Saturday afternoon. Jos and Susan had just walked past the Student's Union Building when out of nowhere Fareed appeared, holding on to a bunch of books from the library. Jos as always thought of an excuse to leave the two alone as she dashed to the toilet.

Josephine: "Susan. I will be back shortly."

Susan had not spotted Fareed. Just as she raised her head, there he was.

Fareed: "Hi Susan, I thought I saw Jos, where has she gone?". Fareed grinned with expectation. Susan: "She's just dashed to the toilet. I guess I have to wait for her here." Susan looked aghast but happy inside. Here was an opportunity to be with Fareed. She knew that Jos would look from a distance and never join the two.

Fareed asked Susan if they could sit on the bench while they waited for Jos. They would remember this bench for a long time as they talked about almost everything from Fareed's parents to how Susan got to the USA. It was clear that these two were headed for something.

Fareed: "How do you feel about going out with someone from another culture," Fareed fired the first salvo".

Susan: "What do you mean? People are people. It doesn't matter where they come from. What matters is whether they love each other and if that is what God wants," Susan spoke like the real preacher. Fareed opened up about his background and how in his community this was very difficult. He spoke about the pressure from his uncle who looked at other races with disdain. These were real fears. And for his society this could mean being ostracised from the family especially that now he was a Christian. To his people this was a lethal combination. Susan could tell from the way Fareed spoke, that this was a

serious matter for him. She began to realise the complexity of
the issues at hand. That it was not just a question of giving in to
love emotions but to the possibility of being isolated once this
became a reality. Her convictions would need to be stronger
and her faith resilient. This was no easy decision.

Susan: "I don't know Fareed. These are very tough issues.
I did not realise that your situation is as difficult as this, Susan
went on. She too had considered some of these issues, but
Fareed had brought up a different dimension.

Susan: "I guess what matters in the end is the faith of the
two, despite where they come from. I suppose the Jesus you
believe in, whom you talked about at that Youth Service,
should be able to see you through some of these difficulties.
I struggle too Fareed. Remember I am from Africa, the dark
continent as they used to call it.

Fareed: "Stop it Susan, Fareed interrupted, that is in the
past and this is now. We are in Cincinnati at University. We are
two people made in the image of God. Whatever decisions we
make is our decision. We are accountable to God and no one
else. If I wanted to marry you Susan that would be my decision
based on what God says and how I feel," Fareed the Preacher
started talking serious business.

Susan: "Stop, (Susan interrupted) are you not being carried
away? We are not even going out and you are talking about
marriage," Susan laughingly looked at Fareed. Here comes
Miss Josephine I guess we better be going,"

Susan was thankful to Jos for showing up at a very crucial
moment while the heat was still on. Fareed stood up.

Fareed: "Ok I guess I better go and take these books back to the library. But Susan, we must talk. I was serious. I will text you. I know a small restaurant by Jefferson Avenue," Fareed shouted as he rushed towards the library.

Josephine: "Eh, you guys looked like you were deep into, well, may be love. I noticed you were lost in conversation. Is he interested?" Jos began to dig deep into what had come out of this conversation. She was keenly interested in seeing these two strike something good. For some reason, Jos respected the two although she felt she could not meet their high moral standards.

Susan: "So, Rome was not built in a day as they say. It's not easy Jos. We are two different people culturally and I wonder whether this can ever work, Susan smiled as she walked towards their flat. But I suppose, I am beginning to understand him and what makes him tick. He sounds very genuine." Josephine: "Well Miss, take the plunge, the next time he throws the big question at you. Sorry, wishful thinking", Jos laughed as she hugged Susan.

CHAPTER 14
BACK IN THE UK

Back in the UK, Melissa could hardly imagine what was happening to her friend Susan. She too had a lot on her plate. Her excitement at her relationship with Keith continued unabated. It was clear from the frequency with which they met that a lot was brewing in their love pot. Melissa had now been in touch with Keith's auntie in Australia. The one who promised to pray for Keith after his dad's birthday. Keith's auntie was very ordinary in her approach to life. Maybe because of her deep relationship with God. She was involved in many charities especially in India. She supported Mother Theresa's Sisters of Hope and many other worthy causes. And because she was coming to visit the UK in the next six months, she assured Melissa that she would meet both. She was excited that her Keith had at last made the decision of his life and in Melissa, found a mature and God-fearing woman.

Melissa could not wait for the day. Arrangements were at an advanced stage, not for the wedding, but for the dowry. You see, according to their culture Melissa's parents had to receive a token of appreciation from their son in law before he was free to marry her. It looked complicated from the outset but fundamentally it meant the sealing of the relationship between the two families. This was news to Brine, Keith's dad when Keith presented the proposal to him and assured him that it was no big deal.

"Do you mean we have to go to her parents, sit on the floor while this ceremony is done. Isn't this asking a bit too much? Why must we grovel on our knees, begging them," dad looked confused. Keith had to put on his solicitor hat, to persuade his dad to appreciate these complexities of culture. He referred to the British royalty and how things were done there as a way of bringing these cultural practices nearer home.

"It's going to be fun dad, it really is, trust me." At this point Melissa started giggling in support of her boyfriend's presentation.

"Is this true Melissa". Have you ever witnessed any of these things?" She nodded before they all agreed that it was something they needed to do and that this would be an opportunity for the two families to meet.

It was not long into their relationship before Keith and Melissa discovered that it would need some skilled navigation to sail through some of the stark differences in their upbringing. For some reason Keith was a spoiled brat, the type that comes from the rich and famous. While his parents were very religious, in that they could walk through the church door with their eyes closed, they had issues. They carried cultural baggage. They were from the aristocracy, living in the very heart of England. Oxford was associated with the prestigious university where Kings, queens, prime ministers, and global leaders passed through its doors. Keith came from the crème de la crème of British society, and this was part of his DNA. Sooner or later, it would raise its ugly head during their relationship. It was a tall order. And Melissa, in all the years she cried to God for someone to marry her did not expect to be answered in this way.

Melissa was always carefree. She was the go girl. Not in a bad way. She believed life was God given and needed to be exploited every step of the way. She was a bundle of joy and had a giggly laugh that made Keith uneasy sometimes, especially when the two were in the company of others. He just could not understand how Melissa could just let go of her smile to all and sundry. He was not used to this and certainly this looked ill-mannered from where he came from. It bothered him at times. He was very careful not to tell her off. Could these be tell -tell signs of what was to come in their relationship, he wondered. And what would be his dad's reaction, let alone his sister and other relatives. He considered this a small matter and decided to ignore it for now.

"Melissa, open the door, its Keith", he had pressed number 5 on the intercom where Melissa stayed. "Keith Who? sorry come in", Melissa giggled as she let Keith in.

This was a two-storey block with six flats, mostly occupied by single professionals. Keith did not frequent Melissa's place as he was careful not to upset her as one who believed in the sanctity of relationships. The times he had come in they watched television or merely talked and laughed until Keith said goodbye. They discussed a lot about their plans regarding marriage and the forthcoming ceremony where the two families would meet to cement their relationship. This day was no different. Melissa said goodbye bye as she stood by the flat door.

"I am going, I will call you tomorrow" Keith reluctantly said his goodbyes.

They held hands and embraced. This time it was different as they clung to each other and let loose their inhibitions for a while. Fortunately Melissa quickly realised that they were nearly going over the precipice, and said softly, "Keith, don't you think we should pray now before you leave". Keith froze. He did not see this coming. He embarrassingly concurred, let go of her and began the most arduous prayer of his life. You see for Melissa this was something she had vowed not to do, letting her feelings overtake her and ruin her honeymoon. She had always been taught that if she kept herself pure from these temptations, she would enjoy her first intimate moment with her new husband with no baggage attached. This was difficult and she was happy that Keith too had realised the importance of this. They finally said goodbye and strangely Keith too was happy there was a way out of this potential temptation.

Chapter 15
The Graduation

George's graduation was a great spectacle. They came from all over the United Kingdom. Everyone associated with Zimbabwe or Africa seemed to descend on this corner of London. Slough was transformed into a hive of congratulations and jubilation. George's parents were tucked at the corner of the little garden where they were having a barbeque. Exhausted but happy that at last their George had made it. Mum remembered his journey through University; the trials and temptations he went through with a little help from her. The stories she had heard about his near misses with girls. *Were they over, she thought? He may have graduated from College, but would he finally make it to finding a woman of his life. She thought back to the times she had tried to impress upon him the need to embrace Godly values, the teaching from the youth groups he attended. Would all this make sense when it came to his decision to find a partner for life? Even now, she was not sure whether George was in a relationship or not. For now, she was happy to celebrate his achievement so far.*

People started to trickle in as the music played. Girls dressed to impress, friends from university and many from the neighbourhood. There was no guest list. All were welcome and this made it difficult to estimate numbers. Food was like manna raining from heaven; drinks, meat. By midnight many had now got their fill of everything. A sprinkling of George's friends was a bit tipsy. They had to be careful because George's dad was very fussy about the young taking alcohol.

Way past midnight, most of the young people decided to change the venue and go downtown to a local disco place. This is where people would let their hair down and do their thing without inhibition. George came to his own when it came to the dance floor. He could wriggle until his waist gave in. Almost! By the time they went to bed it was now morning.

While George was gregarious, life at University had done him a lot of good. Many times he had benefited from the various Christian groups at the university. There students had been reminded of the need to stick to moral absolutes. To do that which will help ensure that they make informed decisions in life. Even at one time when he had a near miss with Charlotte, he still came back to realise the importance of a life of integrity. He always wanted to respect his parents and do what they had always taught him. But now that he had finished Uni what would stop him from living the life that he wanted. Why should he be inhibited by culture or religion? These thoughts began to filter through his psyche. And the longer he entertained them the more he was under pressure to let go. Besides, this was not rural Zimbabwe but Slough just a short distance from downtown London. *Surely, we need to be freer than what our parents went through, he thought.* He decided it was time to talk this over with his girlfriend who did not come to the party because she had just lost her mum's sister.

Catlin was a year ahead of George, so she left before George. She had already secured a part time job by the time George finished Uni. She and her two brothers came from a very deprived family. She had a mind of her own. She was a bit over the top when it came to speaking her mind. She was well known among her friends for calling a spade a spade. When she made up her mind, she could not be persuaded otherwise. Their relationship with George seemed one sided. She was the one to push things and many a times George gave in and ended up leaving his residence to stay with her off campus.

It was when George got a job with one of the computer companies two hours from home that Catlin started pestering George to live with him. And one day unannounced, she left home for George's place. It was the greatest disappointment that she gave to her parents. This had never been done before among their relatives. It was alien to their culture. But this was no longer the village. Young people here seemed to do what they wanted without adhering to certain values. And Catlin had given in to such behaviour. George's dad was not aware for some time about what was happening. He was always the last to know as his wife always wanted to protect him fearing that his heart would not withstand such terrible news. But he eventually got wind of it, and he was devastated. Apparently, George could not withstand Catlin's manoeuvres. And by the time this was news in the neighbourhood, Catlin was already pregnant.

This had become commonplace among young people. Pressure to marry was getting more prevalent and many had given up waiting for the right time and the right person. *Why wait when I can have my baby and perhaps settle for a Council flat on benefits?* For many this had become the plan and many parents found it difficult to persuade their children otherwise. Boys were rendered helpless as they too gave in to the advances of girls. Their answer to the question, "Who will marry me" was simple, *Whoever comes my way in case I miss the boat.* Those who were holding on to values and a relationship with God, seemed to be considered dumb and foolish. This was the new norm and whether you lived in Slough or any other part of the United Kingdom, you were vulnerable and a target. Love predators were on the loose and you ran away from them or you became their prey. And for George and Catlin, it was too late. The noose had caged them in and the best they could do was to conduct a post-mortem before crafting a new future for themselves.

It's not that Catlin was not aware of the need to do it the right way. She had decided to ignore these norms. Her conscience was almost seared and instead of behaving like her mum's buddies, she decided to go against the grain. She was smart in her on way. *Why would she be stuck at home when there was a world out there to be explored. Why should she follow obsolete cultural ways from her distant past in the sticks of Africa? Was this kind of life fit for the twentieth century? All the guys and gals she had met at college, at work, were progressive when it came to relational issues. They were even not just heterosexual but gay and lesbian as well. Hers were very strong views contrary to what her parents believed in.* How she had become this radical heaven knows. But judging by the friends she kept from school to University, there was no doubt that at one point she would be impacted. Unlike George hers was a complete turnaround. Living with someone was no big deal. When she fell in love with George, she knew he was vulnerable from the stories he told about his childhood. He had gone through the Christian mill as it were. And even during the time he was preparing for University, there were a series of focus group sessions in the neighbourhood on marriage. He remembered very well Brother Phillip's famous group discussion when he reported on behalf of the group. These were issues concerning the criteria for finding someone one could marry. This became a foundation for George. And when he eventually went to university, he used this as his spiritual reference point. Now George had lost it. He knew what was right, but he always gave in to the demands from the girls. And when Catlin realised George 's *Achilles' heel*, she pounced on him.

For both George and Catlin, it was not easy to break the news to their parents. Catlin had been away from home all weekend after having gone to visit her friend in the city. Her mum was happy because she had been told her friend was Charlotte, a respected girl within the community. And when Catlin failed to turn up Sunday evening, mum got worried. After a few attempted calls, she decided to text Catlin. Just as she put her mobile down, the landline phone range.

Mum: "Where are you Catlin. We are worried that you haven't arrived yet. Are you working tomorrow?" Mum started off with a barrage of questions, rather relieved that her daughter had phoned.

Catlin: "Mum, I am sorry but I am not coming back tonight. I am not with Charlotte. I am with ... you know my friend George? We have decided to live together, you know", Catlin slowly and carefully justified her absence while announcing what was a bombshell to her parents.

Mum: "Stop it Catlin. Do you know who you are talking to. Do you? Where did you get that idea that you can just tell us you are not coming back? Are you married to him? What happened.?," Catlin's mum began to shout and cry at the same time. *How could her daughter defy her like this? Why? It shows disrespect. What had become of her daughter? What evil had overtaken her? She was now numb and she put the phone down.* She paced up and down in the lounge. She switched on the TV, switched it off again. *Was this the end of marriage prospects for her daughter. Why could she wait a little. Did they not teach her properly? Was it their decision to relocate from Africa to this country? Would she have been better off in Zimbabwe? She imagined how long this had been going on. Were they living like a man and woman? Did it start in College? What kind of a man was her boyfriend who did not respect cultural values? At least he could have come and seek permission from them. Maybe he is white or Indian or Chinese. It was a torrid hour for Priscilla. Had Graham, her husband been there maybe he could have drummed sense into her. But he was away on business.* She would have to wait until the following week. It was not fair to tell him over the phone. Graham sometimes had a very bad temper and anything to do with his children affected his Blood pressure.

Priscilla did not sleep that night. She prayed, read the Bible, searched on google and everything to try and make sense of what had just happened. It was like Catlin had just died and that she would never see her again.

If only Priscilla knew how many parents in the Diaspora were in the same predicament. Parents who had given up on their children. Parents who could not find answers to the complex relationships that were their children's. Many were questioning their decision to seek greener pastures away from home. There was a serious debate going on in many communities. *Was it their decision to leave their motherland which was debatable or was it the grooming of their children? Was the new society to blame. Would this not have happened "back home"? What was the way forward? How could they reconfigure their faith and culture to accommodate what was happening in their adopted home? Why were there young men and women who were properly married and well behaved. How did they do it? What is the formula?*

Instead of it being a children's issue, it was becoming everyone's issue. It needed corporate responsibility to minimise the excesses. This was a complex problem, and it was no use blaming one segment of the population. Both parents and children needed to take responsibility. All the organs of state, churches, religious groups needed to be aware of the elephant in the room. These were difficult times. And unless everyone took control, we would lose future generations.

Catlin never knew that she had opened a Pandoras box when she called her mum that evening.

CHAPTER 16
THE BREAKTHROUGH

Keith was not sure what to put on for the journey to Slough. He was not properly briefed as to what was expected of him on this his first encounter with Melissa's parents. He had heard bits and pieces of stories from Melissa of how her dad could be difficult when it came to her daughter. And this was no ordinary prospective son in law. He was a full-blown Englishman who was, because of TK's decision to abandon the motherland for greener pastures. He sometimes mourned about this, but he had come to realise that unless he changed his attitude, nothing would change. He was in danger of robbing his children a better future. And Melissa was no ordinary child. She was his first-born girl whom he was proud of. She had made him proud. While she was under pressure to go along with the other girls, she stood her ground and stuck to the teaching that she had received from her parents and others in the church fraternity.

All this made it easier for Keith although he did not realise it. He was just as anxious as any boy being introduced to a girl's parents. He had to be at his best. His dad had insisted that he too go with him, but Keith advised against it. Brine 's argument was that someone had to accompany Keith in case something went wrong. Slough was not quite the same as Oxford or Cambridge he argued but he was overruled. The best Keith could do was to put up at his dad's the night before so they could spend some time mulling over the different scenarios of things that could go wrong on the day. Melissa had reminded Keith of the need to be at his best in etiquette, just like he was going to meet the Queen. Sort of!

Since this was an initial visit, TK invited one of his cousins who was a lecturer at University College London. He felt that it was important for Keith to realise that Melissa also came from a highly respected and educated pedigree. This would send a message to Keith's relatives and hopefully endear Melissa's family to the other side. Melissa's mum was the one who was clearly a nervous wreck. She could not sleep the night before. It was like she was the one being introduced to her first boyfriend.

"Why are you doing your hair", TK asked gleefully as she was still locked up in the bathroom for the best part of an hour.

"Stop it TK, don't you realise it's a big day today. I have been pinching myself all morning. I can't believe that we are about to witness history in real time. Do you realise what this means? Our Melissa now has a potential husband. We don't know yet how this is going to end up. All we know is that this boy is our prospective son in law. And that is good enough for me. Even if it is a dream. I don't mind dreaming about it for the rest of my life.," Beatrice just kept talking. TK got the message although he never wanted to show his feelings. A bona fide hypocrite!

Ernest: "Is anyone home?", Ernest TK's cousin was already at the door. He was a bit early, and this took TK by surprise.

TK: "Eh, come in I didn't expect you this early.

Ernest: "TK this is no ordinary day. I did not sleep well last night. I had these visions of Melissa in a white gown shedding tears of joy with women ululating from the side-lines.

TK: "Ernest, you are a bridge too far. We are not there yet. We are still at the start of the journey. It's just an introduction to this boy. They haven't told us of their intentions yet in accordance with our customs." The cultural TK started to give his cousin a lesson in processes and procedures.

Ernest: "TK, where do you think you are? This is Slough mate, in the United Kingdom. There are different rules here. Don't make it difficult for these kids. Let them get on with it. Be careful, you may not live to see your grandchild at the rate you are going," Ernest started teasing TK as he normally did whenever they met.

While there was anxiety in her mum, Keith's dad and even Keith, Melissa remained calm. She made sure all the preparations for the meal afterwards were in place. All she was waiting for was Keith and his friend Jason. Any time soon they would be arriving. The protocol was set in motion and Melissa's young sister Theresa was to receive the guests and escort them to the lounge. Mum and dad would be called downstairs as soon as everyone was there.

As Keith drove into the driveway, he noticed Melissa's car and a few other cars. He was not sure whether these were for Melissa's relatives or just neighbours. Theresa quickly escorted Keith and Jason to the lounge signalling the beginning of the process.

Mum and dad gingerly descended the staircase and for the first time they set their eyes on the two gentlemen. It was difficult to figure out which one was Keith.

Ernest: "Uncle TK, -Ernest began even before the guests were offered a drink- on your right is Jason and on your left is Keith. Keith is Melissa's friend. They are here so that you can meet them. Keith and Jason this is Melissa's mum and dad. Keith shrugged from the sofa. Keith just wait for mum and dad to greet you", Keith embarrassingly sat back.

TK: "Glad to meet you both. We are especially glad to meet you Keith, TK went straight into the introductions. If we were in Zimbabwe, we would have done things differently. But its ok. How are you both?" Both Keith and Jason smiled.

Keith: "We are well thank you. It is a pleasure to meet you too," the two lads spoke in unison.

It didn't take long before everyone looked relaxed. TK made it easier for Keith as he started to ask questions about Keith's legal profession, his near misses with the law when he was in Zimbabwe. It became obvious that they had so much in common when it came to politics. Melissa sat there relieved that at last this was happening. She prayed that this initial visit would go well without a hitch and that her parents would be impressed with her newfound friend. By the time they had lunch, the atmosphere was electric and the meeting of the two cultures for now did not have any hick ups. At least on the surface it didn't.

Jason and Keith said their goodbyes, and as they drove out of the driveway, Keith heaved a sigh of relief.

Keith: "It's done Jason. One step at a time. I love it.," Keith burst into laughter. They are just like us. Of course, there will be differences, but I did not sense anything out of the ordinary", But Melissa's dad looks like a toughie. I am sure in his time he was something. I could tell from the way he threw all those questions at me.", Keith laughed as they headed for the motorway and back to "freedom".

Melissa's parents were pleased in a way. Keith impressed them as someone who was respectful, may be because of his legal background. He tended to be a good listener.

Mum: "Melissa, he looks a bit sophisticated. It is obvious he comes from a very rich family", mum quietly responded looking at her daughter. You could tell she was looking beyond today into a time when the two were together and perhaps in the company of Keith's relatives. *Would she cope? She had lingering questions in her heart which she kept close to her chest. She wanted the best for her daughter. And besides, she had been praying for someone to marry her at the appropriate time.* This seemed to be Melissa's opportunity. Either she grabbed it with open arms or let it slip away from her very eyes, Melissa's mum was convinced that all this was in God's hands. Jesus had promised to take care of her and her family and this was the time to prove Him.

How could an English gentleman fall for a Zimbabwe damsel whose parents came to the country as immigrants. In the real world it did not wash and yet here he was an Oxfordian groomed in the throes of aristocracy. For Keith, this was a big deal. His conviction was solid. Here was someone he loved. Someone he was sure was God given and one who would be his help meet for life. All these processes he was going through were a mere formality. He was just ticking the boxes. They had no effect on the decision he had made. What would happen after, was in God's hands and the two were poised to make it work no matter the obstacles of family and friends. He had seen many couples who had started off well and ended up in a mess. They could not sustain their relationship and succumbed to the whims of their friends and relatives. Many focused on cultural idiosyncrasies instead of their relationship. While these were real, they failed to strengthen their own relationship.

While Melissa was thrilled to have gone past this hurdle, she was still not sure what the rest of the process would be like. She thought of the meeting of the two families in a few months, the preparations for the wedding and of course the penultimate thing, the wedding night. *Was this happening. She thought. Was Keith real? Was he in love? All these thoughts flooded her mind, and it was clear that the journey would be long and winded. She needed strength and much support.* She could not manage some of the apparent contradictions in their background on her own. But God would. Jesus would. All those years of study, training, observing hopefully would pay off. This was no theoretical gimmick. This was life. Any deviation from the core values she was taught in Sunday School or read in the Bible would be costly. Many of her friends had gone through this bumpy road and some fell off the cliff and were wounded for life.

CHAPTER 17
THE IRAQI CONNECTION

There was so much happening in Susan's life that she hardly found time to call Melissa. She knew Melissa was concerned about her newfound friend. So much had happened since. The struggle to find who would marry Susan was beginning to ebb away with what was happening to her relationship with Fareed. This was still a nightmare. How on earth could this lad appear in her life at this time in the USA? She never imagined that she would be thinking or contemplating marrying an Iraqi man so handsome and kind. This was anathema in her country, let alone her village back home. But it was beginning to be real. She was staring something strange in her face. And for Melissa this would be unheard of. Susan was very careful not to share much about her relationship. She was fortunate that her roommate was like a black box. She kept things in her chest too. But of course, walls have eyes and sooner or later the cat would be let out of the bag. Their love was so strong that people were bound to ask. And they did.

It started at church. There was love in the air and little by little, news began to trickle in the ears of the leadership. It was not difficult for people to identify Fareed. He was the lad who gave that powerful testimony during the Youth Service. But Susan was less conspicuous. A few had seen her pushing a lady in a wheelchair a few times but that was all. An unsung hero who preferred to remain in the background. But not any longer. There was now a new song. "Susan and Fareed are going out". That was the beginning of their public journey of love. There was no going back. This was a test in the viability of cross-cultural relationships. They were not the first nor were they going to be the last.

The arrival of Susan's parents in the USA at the invitation of her uncle and auntie, supported by their church, was going to be the real ice breaker. They had never been abroad before and this was their first time to meet their relations in a strange land.

There was excitement on the day the call came through from the American Embassy for an interview to determine whether they were eligible for a USA visa. It felt like the sky had given in and for the first time their destiny was truly in their hands. "Please can you hurry, or we will be late, you never know what these Americans are looking for. You may be disqualified for being late," Dickson almost shouted at Marble his wife who was still in the bathroom making some finishing touches to her hair. She did not answer back but quickly brushed her hair and dashed for the car. Dickson and Marble had not been fortunate enough to travel abroad although they were seasoned teachers at a local secondary School. They had entertained foreign visitors, either at school or at their local church. So, for them the opportunity to visit the USA where their daughter was studying was a blessing from God. It was an opportunity of a lifetime considering they were now due for early retirement.

Parking near the embassy was always a nightmare following a beefing up of security defences outside because of the terrorist scares worldwide. So, they had to risk parking in the avenues, notorious for marauding thieves who broke into cars to grab whatever they could. The appointment was at half past two in the afternoon. The reception area was jammed with all and sundry seeking interviews. They had to wait until their name were called. This was a one-to-one interview by the reception window. It was not confidential as those in the reception area could hear what was being said. Just before their turn, was a group of young men. Their spokesperson was asked why they wanted to travel. 'We are musicians, and we are going to tour different churches singing as we go'. 'How do I know you are all singers. May be some of you want to take advantage and abscond.' the officer retorted. The officer came out to the reception where all the boys were and asked them to sing so he could spot those who were taking advantage. The boys nearly brought the house down. Their voices were so synchronised and melodical that other officers came down to witness. They were issued their visas straight away.

This raffled Dickson and Marble, making them very anxious. The officer asked them a few questions about the uncle who was inviting them and the church acting as their guarantor. They were asked whether they had any other relative in the USA. He looked both in the face and said "Congratulations, you have been granted a visa. Enjoy your stay." The official from the Embassy relayed the good news. Dickson and Marble both froze and quickly realised that their dream had come true and would now be able to be with their only daughter Susan. Marble took over the driving seat as she was the more stable when it came to such adrenalin generating decisions. They were now only a few weeks away from flying to Oklahoma.

Susan was excited to hear that mum and dad were granted visas. At last, she would be reunited with them after three years. While she was excited, she began to think of what had happened to her and Fareed. The relationship had suddenly mushroomed out of control. Her uncle did not yet know about it. Each time he phoned to ask how she was she was not bold enough to share about her budding love life. Besides, you don't normally talk about such things to your uncle. Even mum at home occasionally tried to find out what was happening in her life, but Susan would not budge. Now it seemed the die was now cast. One way or the other this would come up during their three months stay. And God had brought Fareed into her life for such a time as this.

Where would she start? Not that her parents objected to her finding someone she could marry. That was to be expected. But to hear that the person she was going out with and thinking of marrying was not black or Zimbabwean, this would test her parents' tolerance levels. They had been brought up to see the world in black and white. Literally. They had experienced so much racism and bigotry in their lives that any association with the enemy's camp was frowned upon. This is where Susan had to dig deep into her faith and seek to find answers there. She was convinced that left on her on she would not be able to fight this battle. She could see her Fareed being swept away by the storms of cultural intolerance because of the colour of his skin and his oriental demeanour. Her parents visit would now take a different dimension. She decided that before they arrived, she would need to persuade her uncle and aunt to buy her idea of going out with Fareed. She thought it wise to quickly introduce him to them in the hope that they would embrace him and be the go between when her parents arrived. Besides, her parents would most likely listen to the uncle since he was responsible for bringing them to the USA.

Josephine could not believe it when Susan told her that her parents had been granted visas and that they were preparing to visit within a few weeks.

Josephine: "Have you told your mum about your newfound lover, Susan,- Jos kicked off the interrogation- I don't know how you do it in your culture, but I prefer talking to mum first. She will in turn neutralise dad. You can phone her or send her an email or something. But on second thoughts, this may backfire. It's better to talk to her face to face."

Susan: "Jos, it's not easy. I think I will talk to her when she arrives and perhaps share this with auntie," Susan said with a grin on her face. This discussion went on for some time until they agreed that Susan does what is acceptable in her culture.

It took Fareed some time for him to realise how serious his relationship with Susan had become. Their eyeball-to-eyeball encounter at a restaurant along Jefferson avenue was a real love experience. As they sat at table waiting for the waiter to appear, it was irresistible for the two to intimately let their feelings run riot. While there was no audible voice from heaven, there was an aura of conviction on the table that they were meant for each other. Months of prayer and seeking seemed to be paying off.

Fareed: "Susan, Fareed softly whispered, looking straight into her eyes. I don't know but, you know, never mind." Susan could tell from the welling in Fareed's eyes that something was simmering.

Susan: "I am listening, Susan started giggling and quickly held her composure as she realised that this was not the time to crack jokes. She was trying hard to camouflage her feelings. Her heartbeat had reached unacceptable levels. There was a mixture of passion and conviction she had never felt before. Fareed held her hand across the table while stroking it gently.

Fareed: "I am desperate for you Susan. I love you very much. I know I have kind of said it before, but right now I am full of it. He smiled as he released her hand as the waiter stood there perplexed. Sorry, we are ready to order now", Fareed quickly gained his composure as he got back to food business. This was the quickest meal order they had ever made. Simple. Combo chicken and shrimp stir fry. As the waiter disappeared into the kitchen, Susan just let go. She was crying with her head on the table. It looked embarrassing as some guests started to look across, wondering what had happened.

Fareed leaned over, "Susan, come on, please. It's alright. Please." He did not realise what he had just done. For Susan to witness such outpouring of love from Fareed was unbelievable. He did not realise how many hours on end Susan had spent thinking, praying for the future she thought was unkind to her. Was this the beginning of a new life? Was this what being in love was all about? Was this finally the answer to her prayers? She was overwhelmed and could not pull herself together.

Susan: "Sorry Fareed but thank you. You don't know how I have felt for you from the day we met in the lab. I knew then that something had happened. I was not sure. Now it's for real. I love you too Fareed. It's odd -she began to laugh- a Zimbabwean girl having a crash at an Iraqi Mr handsome." They all began to laugh. It was very sentimental to watch and for the other guests it did not make sense that one minute she was crying and now both laughing away. If only they knew.

The food was sumptuous, a far cry from what they were used to at the College canteen. Susan spoke about her parent's impending visit and how she was not sure how she would break the news to her mum.

Susan: "Fareed are you going to tell your parents about us, or have you told them already?", Susan began to seek solace from Fareed.

Fareed: "Not really, I am a bit scared. I don't know how they will respond. You know my parents, especially my uncle., he went on.

Susan: "I remember you told me about his disdain for other races. I am sure once he meets me, he will realise that I am special. A princess of sorts, eh! Susan giggled as they walked along the boulevard on their way to the campus."

Fareed: "Seriously, I must figure out how? Pray for me please. My sister doesn't know either and maybe I should sound her first before I dive into the deep waters."

It was clear that both had issues with their parents, and they needed to carefully navigate these murky waters. The good thing was that they were convinced they had made the right decision. The challenge now was transforming the decision into something tangible. They needed to overcome the obstacles and reach their destination. They were both in their final year. There was need to concentrate on their studies instead of being preoccupied by this love thing.

By the time Susan got to her room, Joss was already dozing off. She had waited to hear the juicy news about their night out. For Jos, this was something she had hoped for ever since Susan mentioned Fareed's name.

Josephine: "Look at you, Jos started hugging Susan. You look different already. Tell me, how was it, how did he treat you. He is a gentleman isn't he." Jos was anxious to hear from Susan.

The story left Jos speechless. She could sense that Susan finally had been bowled over. They were indeed officially "love birds" on campus. She was witnessing history being made under her nose. Her imagination ran riot. *She knew this was not going to happen soon. The marriage, wedding. May be years down the line and may be not if this Jesus Susan always talked about did not suddenly turn up to wrap up this whole episode called life. How she wished she was able to witness the tale of these two cultures coming together one day. And if this was replicated across the world, what a world it would be. African, Chinese, Indian, Japanese, English, all together as one. Josephine had no solutions, but only wishes, hopes.*

Susan: "Jos, we had a fab night. The food, the place, the atmosphere. And of course, Fareed was such a gentleman. I didn't realise that the best gentlemen come from the Middle East! For once I became one with him, if you know what I mean. This is real Jos. I am in love," she began to quietly sob.

Josephine: "Come on Sue – Jos went across the sofa and wrapped her hands around her. It's ok. Isn't this what you have been praying for. Your Jesus has finally answered your prayer, Susan. It's time to celebrate! Look at me. What hope have I got." Jos too began to cry.

There was a feeling of release and contentment as they both realised that love changes everything. Race, culture pale into insignificance when there is an overflow of real love. And this was what was happening between Susan and Fareed. Jos and Sue had a cuppa and retired to bed. What a day for Susan.

CHAPTER 18
LOVE HURTS

Since leaving the diplomatic service, Ahmed Hassan, Fareed' dad remained in the Gulf region as Chief Executive of one of the Big Oil Firms in the Middle East. His Chemical engineering degree came in handy when he left Baghdad after the war. It was not difficult for him to sponsor Fareed to study in the USA. He had great hopes for his only son, and it was no surprise that he too had chosen to do Chemical engineering. The plan was to find a lucrative job for his son once he finished university. He prayed to Allah that he would find a religious Arab girl who would become his daughter in law.

After Fareed's love encounter with Susan, he knew that the struggle had only begun. He began to imagine what his parents' response would be once he told them that he had found a girl from Africa. He sometimes had sleepless nights over this. Not because he had lost trust in the God he had now embraced, but because reality was looking at him in the face. There were real obstacles that he had to face and go through. His parents, his uncle, his friends back home and in the Arab community in the USA. Not to mention Susan's parents who were soon to visit America. He decided to take the bull by its horns. To do this he had to pray to his God and be specific about what interventions he was looking for. One of the things he prayed for was to ask God to give him and Susan strength to withstand any negative insinuations over their relationship. To be able to keep together even when the going got tough. Another significant prayer was for God to destroy the cultural wall that seemed to divide communities and dictate to them what they should or should not do. He realised that his newfound faith in Jesus was non-discriminatory, and marriage was a cross border thing as far as God was concerned. This was his comfort and as the days went by, he would hold on to it.

One evening just as he came out of the library, he rang his uncle in the Middle East. He was going to make this very short. He had one item on his agenda. Susan.

Fareed: "Hi uncle, Salaam ".

Uncle: "Eh Fareed, what is happening. Are you ok? Oh, my beloved cousin. Don't tell me you have bumped into a beautiful Arab girl in the USA.," uncle started bubbling with joy and expectation. Uncle Mahmoud was gregarious, joyful, and full of life for his age. He had a soft spot for Fareed as the only boy born to his nephew. He was overprotective. This time he did not know what Fareed was up to.

Fareed: "Uncle just called to check on you. Are you alright? I don't have much airtime, I thought I would tell you that I have a girlfriend now. I met her here at University. She is the best thing that has ever happened to me uncle."

Uncle: "Hold your horses Fareed. First things first. Is she from this part of the world or are her parents immigrants in

America from here.? Fareed started coughing as if suddenly he was suffering from manful. He nearly choked as his predictions came true over the phone. He had to think quickly. A prayer would do before he answered as this could make or break not just this conversation but the prospects of Susan being accepted in the family.

Fareed: "Uncle, I have no airtime now. I will phone again. Just wanted you to know what's happening here. Are you coming for the graduation? I will let you know everything when you come.

Uncle: "Fareed, thank you my nephew's son. Send me a photo of your friend please.

Fareed: "Bye uncle", Fareed quickly hung the phone and sighed a huge relief happy that he had not revealed much to spoil the conversation.

Susan was wondering what had happened to Fareed after trying to reach him on the phone. That was the night he was talking to his uncle. She had been trying to get hold of him. She was excited that her mum and dad had boarded their plane in Harare, Zimbabwe flying via Dubai, Amsterdam, Minneapolis St Paul and on to Cincinnati. She could not hold her joy and trepidation as this visit had become critical following his relationship with Fareed.

Fareed: "Susan, sorry, I was on the phone with my great uncle. Remember him, the one I am afraid of when it comes to his attitude towards relationships like ours",

Susan: "Fareed, before you finish, mum and dad are in the air now and they will be arriving in two days' time. Fareed, do you know what this means. You will now be able to meet them and hear their "verdict". Not that it matters because it is all about us and not them. We are what Jesus wants us to be."

Fareed: "I am happy for you Susan, but do you know what my uncle said even before I told him I was in love with you? He asked if I had met a beautiful Arab woman from the Middle East. That is annoying. He always thinks about tribes and ethnicity.

Susan: "Fareed don't be silly. That is what he was brought up to think. Sometimes it takes ages for people to change and maybe he will never change but if we do it right, this may strike a chord with him and others in your family and mine. We could be the real pioneers," Susan started giggling over the phone.

Fareed: "Susan, I hope you are right". I will see you at church tomorrow. I must go back to the library. Love you".

These encounters had become routine for these two lovebirds. They either sent text messages or just conversations on end over the phone as the bonding became deeper and deeper. They began to appreciate the challenges of living in the Diaspora; now it was beginning to affect their love life. They imagined how easy it would have been if they were in their respective countries not bound by culture or religious persuasion. They appreciated the fact that even their parents too were bound to struggle to make sense of some of the decisions they were on the verge of making. Marriage had suddenly become complex as it was not as straightforward as they thought. Their decision went beyond the confines of their love relationships. Family, close relations and even the community was affected. The different attitudes of people would make it harder to navigate their relationship. They never saw this coming when they decided to be serious. *They imagined what it would be like when they officially got married. They thought about the impact on their children. How would they fit into the community? Would they survive the labelling that goes on especially when it comes to the Middle East? This was not for now but the future. While this was going on, Susan was busy thinking about her parents who would be arriving in a few hours.*

From the time Jade was chucked out from Tino's house she remained bitter. She was not in love with Tino, but his mother thought otherwise. She had begun building relationships with her son's kith and kin when this happened. Memories of what happened to her when she got pregnant at College were slowly waning. And then this. A reminder that she was not quite welcome and that somehow, she did not belong. She may have borne a black child but that was it. It pained her that she was being defined by the colour of her skin. No one seemed to want to appreciate her as a human being. If only they could peep into her heart and see the love, compassion, and kindness there. She knew she could not win the battle. She felt sorry for her little princess. *What will happen to her princess when she grows up in a community with mothers who care less for someone who is not their own, Jade thought*

While Tino did not appreciate what his mother had done to Jade, he could not freely express his sentiments. He knew that for her mum white girl love was forbidden. You just did not go there. Mum was brought up to shun whites. Not because of some courage but out of fear. She had never resolved her inferiority complex issue. She had a chip on her shoulder, and the only way to overcome this was to pretend that she was stronger than the other side. Sadly, it was fake. It was a cover up. Somehow, she had managed to hoodwink her children and others in her community. Her relocation to the UK, meant that she had to intensify such hate to survive and keep to herself. She never wanted to integrate except at church where she always played a saint through her plastic smile which fooled very few.

Mum: "Tino, remember you are not a white person. So, these careless invites of white girls to my house must stop. I felt very offended to come home and see that girl of yours in this house," Tino's mum Cecilia began to blurt at her son drowning in the sofa watching the X Factor. You should remember where you come from and what these people are like in their country. As for me, I will not sink so low. I have my pride. Besides, there are many black girls around. Joanna, Christine, Merle, Tafadzwa, Tariro, I am sure you know that.," she went on.

Tino just looked at his mother and quietly responded. "Mum, I thought you were a Christian. Doesn't the Bible say there is neither Jew nor Gentile, and there is neither Jew nor Gentile, neither slave nor free, nor is there male and female, for you are all one in Christ Jesus" Galatians 3:28 NIV. Why all this discrimination then. Is God not for the rich, the poor, blacks, whites, Latinos.?", -Tino just hit the nail on the head-. Mum, Jade is just a friend from College. She is not my girlfriend. She has been through a lot in her short life. She got pregnant in high school and had to stop school until she gave birth to have baby boy. And do you know who did that. A boy from Sudan, who, once he knew she was pregnant, did not want to know anything about her. Her parents were bitter and at one time removed her from the house because of what she had done. And just as she was about to resolve her issues through meeting people who could help her including myself, my mother joins the bandwagon, and you too judged her before you could understand where she came from.

Mum it is painful. I wish you had stopped to think before you unceremoniously chased her away; How embarrassing. All this in the name of culture? How do you pick the pieces of such a bruised peach? I don't know mum. I am not condemning you, but I am trying to give you the full story of the girl you did not want to see in this house. I wished you had come in and listened and perhaps prayed for her. You are not alone mum. Many of my age group from Africa are beginning to realise that whatever happened back home has really affected you, our parents. But we are here now. We need to talk about this because for now this is home. This is what we know. Either we integrate or we go downhill and lose our identity."

Mum: "Tino, stop it. Thanks for the lecture. I am sorry about your Jade; I did not realise that that was where she came from. Poor child. But I am sure you can understand what I did. Seeing a girl in my house with you was a bit too much. You know I have always wanted the best for you. We have always had a sense of morality. I am not saying I was suspicious of something, but this could be the beginning of something not good.," mum began to ease a bit as she reflected on what she had done without apologising to her son.

Across the immigrant community, these draconian measures were felt in most homes. These homes became islands in a country and community that tended to allow its children to express themselves. They took pride in their children who were in the main very polite and respectful unlike the indigenous children. But there was always a need to balance the two extremes. Tino's mother although she claimed to be a Christian tended to act before she thought. This was a dangerous risk. She was fortunate to have a son who was always calm and composed and showed some maturity in the manner he spoke and responded to issues. They nicknamed him the professor at college as he spent hours with older students discussing real issues of politics, culture. No wonder why Jade had found solace in Tino and their friendship was not tainted with erotic thoughts as some relationships were. She had somehow found somebody in whom she could confide in.

CHAPTER 19
THE NET CLOSES IN

If there was one person Melissa was keen to talk to regarding her rollercoaster relationship, it was Brother Phillip. His focus group sessions regarding marriage were a defining moment for her. It was at these meetings that Melissa and many other young people were able to reflect on themselves and the implications of the decisions they were going to make in life. Melissa clearly remembered her report back at one of these sessions. She was touched by how the other peers reacted to it which gave her hope that one day she would eventually meet her Mr Right. Now was her moment with her Keith in the bag as it were, a gift from God.

Brother Phillip and his family apparently had left the neighbourhood. He was now working as a probation officer in Scotland. Wherever he was, she was keen to let him know about what was happening in her life. Unknown to Melissa, Brother Phillip had been killed on the motorway. Apparently, his car broke done and while it was parked on the hard shoulder brother Philip was hit by a passing truck as he tried to call the Car breakdown people. It left his family devastated and many in the church especially young people, mourned him for days.

Melissa was devastated. The very person she wanted to witness her wedding was gone. This reminded her of the momentary nature of life and that while there was so much to look forward to, death too was in the queue waiting to take people to their destiny. This in a sense brought everything into its proper perspective. It made Melissa realise that while marriage was noble and many like her were desperately looking for someone to spend their life with, life was only a journey that could have an abrupt end.

Keith had his moments too. He sometimes slipped into moments of silence even during a conversation. Like this day out in the park with Melissa.

Melissa: "Keith, what are you thinking? You seem to be in another world. It worries me. You have to stop this daydreaming." Melissa noticed. They had just been out walking in the park before they headed for home. As they sat in the car, with her huddled in Keith's arms, she could sense that he was not there. At least in spirit.

Keith: "I am here. There is so much to think about. It's not easy for me sometimes. Having gone through this before and all what I went through at the last minute, I don't know whether this time it will happen.

Melissa: "Come on Keith. You believe in God, don't you? Isn't this what we have been doing since, praying for God to guide and protect us. I don't think you should be anxious. What about me? Do you know how many people have warned me about what happened to you and think that I am taking a gamble? Mum was the one who rebuked me when I was sharing my concerns about what people were saying. And she had a point. When we bring our relationship to Jesus, he will take care of the rest. By being anxious we change nothing. And there are many people who are hoping that we don't make it. They are jealous. We cannot stop them. Such people will always be there, and it is for us to resist their plans and forge ahead.", Melissa was showing the kind of mature girl she was. While this was a sensitive and delicate subject, she needed to assure her lover that she was right behind her. That the past was gone forever and there was a new life with so much in store.

When Auntie from Australia heard that Keith and Melissa were serious about marriage and that they were now beginning to plan for their wedding, she decided to fly to the UK. Brine had briefed her about Melissa's visit and Keith's visit to TK's family. This was now serious stuff. It was no longer who will marry whom, but when. It required some planning as this would involve Brine's relations dotted all over the world.

Auntie 's flight was delayed. Melissa, Keith and Brine had all been waiting for her at the airport for an hour. Melissa wasn't sure why she had come. Keith insisted. He wanted to break the ice immediately and avoid protocol when he got home. Besides, auntie was always on his side and as a woman of prayer she wanted the best for him and his girlfriend. Brine was restless as they waited. Sometimes when it came to family issues, he couldn't help thinking about his late wife. He wished she was present to witness what was happening to her only son. But he always reminded himself that this was God's will.

Keith: "Hey, look dad that's auntie waving." Keith ran towards the exit doors from where the passengers were streaming towards the arrival hall. Melissa and Keith waved back, smiling.

Keith: "Auntie, this is Melissa. Remember from dad's birthday party? She is the one I have been talking about."

Auntie just went for Melissa, hugging kissing and sobbing at the same time. It was very moving as she looked at Brine.

Auntie: "Good to see you Melissa. Welcome."

Melissa: "Oh, thank you. That is very kind of you. Did you have a safe flight?

Auntie: "Yes thank you Melissa. Oh Brine, I am forgetting you, my brother."

She hugged Brine and kissed him as they both had tears running down their cheeks. They pulled her small case to the car park. This was the close family and whatever was to be planned these four were in charge and responsible. The wedding process had begun, and Keith and Melissa were finally on the way to becoming man and wife. A dream coming true, and an answer to Melissa's lifelong question, "Who will Marry me?

Auntie Doreen (Dee as family called her) was immaculate. She had great poise a typical Oxfordian, but unassuming. From her demeanour you could not tell that she came from the aristocrats of middle England. As she always said, 'Jesus broke me and made me who I am'. She was not a religious fanatic. She was a humble lass who had found a new relationship with her Maker. Her whole life was affected. She seemed to ooze Jesus in her DNA. Prayer had become something of a routine and habit. She talked to God just like she was breathing fresh air from a pond. So you can understand her joy and excitement when she for the first-time hugged Keith's wife -to -be after praying for this for as long as she could remember. In fact, Keith's mum before she died had asked untie Dee to pray for Keith. All she wanted was for Keith to have a relationship with God, and for him to find an equally spiritually battle-hardened Proverbs 31 woman. It took years of prayer and faith riddled with setbacks and stresses, as the years rolled on without sight of the bride to be. Her being in Australia meant that at least she was removed from the scene and would occasionally hear from Keith and Brine. It was all over now. Melissa, who too had struggled over the years to find God's match for her was now a whisker away. It was happening in real time and Auntie Dee just sobbed inside.

The drive home from the airport was interrupted by sighs of, 'Melissa, thank you, you don't know what this means to me', as Auntie Dee kept stretching her neck to get a glimpse of Melissa who was sitting at the back beside Keith.

Auntie: "You are an answer to prayer, love. I will tell you the story one day. I am a bit overwhelmed now."

Brine: "Here we go again", Brine stared at Auntie Dee. He knew that once she started talking about the past there would be no stopping and she would end up crying incessantly. It happened before and he did not want to spoil her home coming and only focus on Keith's great news.

Melissa was spellbound when she heard a bit of Auntie Dee's struggle as she prayed for Keith. This was clear confirmation that God had prepared Keith for her. There was now no doubt in her mind that Keith was the one for her. It was not coincidence but God's plan. She couldn't wait to share with her parents this daylight miracle. She thought these things happened in the past but here she was, being the recipient of God's goodness in her life.

As Melissa reflected on her journey, she remembered many of her friends who had given up mid-stream. They lost focus and some let go the little faith they had in the God who alone could make it happen. For Melissa it was a game of patience. There were times she bumped into young, handsome men who appeared genuine from outside and yet they were counterfeit fruit from inside. Sometimes it was difficult to decipher. There were many near misses when she almost fell into the trap like some of her friends but at the last minute was rescued. This had become a frustrating ongoing experience, and many had fallen by the wayside and lived in regret all their lives. For Melissa, a consistent experience of God and his values shone through each time she was discouraged and felt nothing good would come out of her relationships. But for her, the tipping point was when the community organised focus group sessions for young men and women in the Village Hall where these issues were candidly addressed. It seems like young men and women needed a platform where they could air their views, concerns, and frustrations in the presence of their peers. These sessions were so beneficial that many changed course as a result or found friends to share with in their community; Melissa being one of them. And here she was on the verge of tying the knot with Keith.

Brine: "Doreen what do you think about her, I mean your first impression?", Brine began to interrogate his sister as if there was any plan B. All he wanted was a confirmation from his sister that Melissa was the real deal.

Doreen: "Eh, I have only arrived, you should give me your assessment first. But I must say that there is something in that girl. I mean spiritually. Even when I saw her briefly at your party last year, it seemed like our spirits locked horns. I love her. She is my kind of girl.," Doreen unconsciously rumbled on with excitement.

Brine: "Hold your horses, I thought you said you had only met her. What's this now. You seem to have known her for ages,"

Brine smiled feeling satisfied that the confirmation from her sister had finally arrived. They continued sipping coffee on the balcony overlooking the Lido lake. Ducks swimming in twos seemed to be rehearsing what the two were imagining about the wedding in a years' time. As the sun set in the horizon on a beautiful summer day, it looked like this was the end of the search for Keith and the beginning of a new dawn.

And all this time, no one mentioned Mellissa's ethnicity. This seemed to have paled into insignificance. For now, it was only thoughts of a beautiful bride draped in integrity. That was enough and Keith wanted it that way. Besides, these two were the closest relatives who mattered. He wanted to keep it that way.

The plan was that the wedding would take place in Oxford at the Cathedral. Since there were many guests coming from abroad, Keith would oversee the visa applications especially for Melissa's old auntie who had to be at the wedding from Zimbabwe. The other guests were from the USA and New Zealand and Brine's brother from the Middle East. And of course, Melissa's old buddy Susan and her friend travelling from the United States. Everyone looked forward to that important day in the life of Melissa and Keith.

CHAPTER 20
IT IS NO SECRET

Susan had just arrived home a few hours before driving to the airport to pick mum and dad. She had a missed call and a text; both were from Melissa. The message read: 'It's all systems go Sue. We are getting married on the 26th of April next year'. Susan rushed in and threw herself on the little sofa in her room. She burst into song, stood up, paced up and down, sat down and started crying. Her friend had made it after years in the wilderness of uncertainty. There was indeed a God who remembers out there after all these years. Melissa's prayer had been heard. There was hope for her too, Susan thought. *She thought of her and Fareed and how things were now shaping up; although they still had a long way to go. But who knows, she thought. Once we are ready, what prevents us from being together and tie the knot?* She quickly went to the bathroom to freshen up and she was off to the airport to meet her aunt from Zimbabwe.

Susan's aunt could see the plane taxiing on the shorter runway carefully docking into the main building. She felt numb as the seat belt sign was turned off. This was a far cry from what she was used to in the village. Here she was on USA soil not quite ready to meet her niece. What a journey, what a country. One of the stewardesses quickly came to mama Simango's aid. "Hello mum, we will now take you to the immigration counter before you are joined with your family". She laughed a little and in her own language mattered some words. *If only this girl knew that I have no clue where I am going, she thought.* The immigration official was very polite. He examined her documents, asked her to look straight into the camera and stamped her passport. She was escorted to the arrival hall where the whole tribe was waiting. There was pandemonium, screams and ululation as they all mobbed her like angry bees in search of food.

"Welcome mama welcome, Oh I can't believe it." Susan began sobbing, her thoughts tinged with fear as she had so much to talk about. Her auntie would soon be her saviour as she presented her newfound boyfriend to her parents. It was easier going through auntie as was the situation back home in Zimbabwe. They quickly drove off from the airport on to the interstate highway. And in one hour would be home. What a day.

Auntie was on a two-year visa but would only stay for six months. This was long enough as this came within the time when Susan would graduate from University. It was a historic time and a rare occasion for the family to be together. Susan's parents were already in the country and looking forward to Susan's graduation.

Meanwhile, Fareed stayed in his room on campus. His excitement was tinged with fear too as he contemplated what would happen when Susan finally broke the news to her parents.

Susan: "Hey Fareed, auntie is here. She is ok but still

recovering from the jet leg., Don't worry, all will be well. She is very understanding. I will have to figure out when I can break the good news to her. Mum and dad will have to accept it as they respect untie.," Susan kept on trying to reassure Fareed.

Fareed: "No probs, God is on our side", Fareed tried to put a spiritual spin to his conversation. No doubt he believed it but so much would have to be in place before the full package was ready for delivery. He thought of his uncle, his parents, and other relatives, not to mention some of his Iraqi friends.

It was late in the evening when Susan caught up with Fareed. Susan threw herself on to Fareed. It was a very emotional hug. Crying and sobbing at the same time.

Fareed: "Hey what's the matter, I thought you said you were happy auntie came. Has anybody upset you?" Fareed spoke like the man in charge.

Susan: "I just feel so emotional looking at you and the hurdles before us. Sorry, sometimes I appear childish I know," Susan giggled her way out of her emotional outburst. They laughed excitedly walking towards Susan's room. He said goodbye and ran towards the men's residential building. What a day for both. It was back to the grind Monday morning. The final exams were now beckoning, and they would soon complete their studies.

Fareed was intelligent and ambitious. He expected to come up with a first in his B.Sc. honours degree in Chemical Engineering. And because of his father's position in the Middle East, he expected to land a very lucrative job at one of the Petroleum companies. This could mean that eventually he would move to the Middle East with his family when they got married. But it was still a long way, but Fareed kept dreaming.

The next few weeks were a nightmare for Susan and Fareed. There was little time to catch up let alone to plan for the next phase of their meet the family tour. The good thing was that they knew this was the end of University and could look forward to the world out there. Graduation was still in the distance and the plans for it were not as grand since it was left to their parents to organise such. Fareed however had the most headache as he had not begun to make in rods into his family regarding his relationship with Susan. The cultural differences were a mountain to climb, so he thought, and he needed wisdom and some sprinkling of grace and humility.

Susan's uncle and auntie knew they would be stuck at home most of the time during mum's visit. Not because she insisted but because this was a carefully planned trip and they had made the necessary arrangements at their workplaces. Uncle George looked agile for a man who was in the twilight of his life. Nearly sixty. Auntie Marble although younger looked a little rusty for her age following her chemotherapy treatment. Her face was the bright light of her demeanour. She sparked each time someone talked to her about the dreadful illness which had invaded her upper body but not her soul. She had an unconquerable faith which at times could move mountains. Her husband, a gentleman by all accounts lived a life of extreme dedication to the Jesus he loved. His faith meant that Marble could always rely on George. He had a rigorous daily prayer schedule. He believed in constant communication with his God early each morning. And this meant that he experienced a certain vitality that men of his age would die for.

Uncle George was one person who was so close to Susan. He was there for her and was responsible for bringing her into the United States of America. He had become her mentor. Not many at University realised how strong Susan's foundation was. And even when she encountered incessant peer pressure on arrival on campus, what she learnt from Uncle George never escaped her. The Diaspora became a testing ground for the many truths she had learnt over the years. He was more of an example. His concern was not with someone's culture but their relationship with God. All else was insignificant. And here he was, very soon to be introduced to Susan's love of her life. From Iraq! Welcome to the land of opportunity.

Fareed's parents were already planning for their son's graduation. Qatar was several hours away from the USA. And as an executive person working in the oil industry he did not anticipate the usual problems. A former Ambassador, a graduate of one of America's prestigious universities, Yale and Harvard. He wanted the best for his only son. A lucrative career, a good life and most importantly a great woman who would mother their Arabic heritage. He used to play an imaginary game called Where will our daughter be married? pointing randomly on any country on the map of the Middle East. They would blindfold each other and randomly point at a spot on the map. In many cases, Jordan and the UAE were victims. Rarely did their fingers point outside the confines of the Middle east. They believed

Allah would not let their son wonder away from home even though he had had expressed interest in following Jesus Christ. At least he would be reasonable enough to graze nearer home where tradition was as old as the foundations of the world.

Ahmed, Fareed's uncle still remembered his conversation with his Fareed, which ended abruptly. He was not quite sure why Fareed did not tell him about his acquaintance in the USA if there was one. His response was vague, and he wanted to follow up this lest Fareed could be misled into going for anyone who had no Arabic roots thereby creating complications for the family.

At least Susan and Fareed had settled the matter. They loved each other and the pending intros were mere formalities. They had decided to stick together no matter what! And Fareed did not realise that in Uncle George he would find a willing warrior ready to stand by him all the way.

Time went by slowly for Susan and Fareed. The exams were now past them and it was time for reality to set in. In a few weeks they would both graduate.

The stage was set. Fareed's mum and dad were to fly in through New York to Cincinnati. Uncle Ali hoped to come too, but it was doubtful. There were not many from Susan's family to represent the family except her uncle and auntie. Following the ceremony, a big bash was planned to celebrate both these great achievements. But Susan and Fareed had already decided that it was better to postpone the good news until after their graduation. They did not want to risk it.

CHAPTER 21
THE GRADUATIONS

The hall was packed but many people were still coming in when the academic procession started walking towards the platform. Susan and her fellow graduates were already sitting on the stage. There was a sea of dignitaries who had been invited from other universities. Susan's parents, uncle and auntie and the big auntie from Zimbabwe were perched right in front for a better view, since big auntie's eyes always let her down. The proceedings were typical for such occasions. And then came the capping of the graduates. As each student went up to the podium there were loud cheers. Some received inaudible ones as they were scantily represented.

Susan started walking towards the President of the University who was capping them and as she received her scroll there was ululating of a kind never witnessed in any academic function before. Big auntie's shrill and shouting brought excitement to the guests and students.

A few friends of Susan right at the corner started chanting: 'Susan, Susan! and the whole place erupted for a few seconds. The president was caught by surprise, but he let it be and just said, 'Thank you' and went on to call the next student.

Since Fareed's graduation was the following week, he cuddled himself at the back of the hall. *His imagination went wild. Here he was witnessing his best friend's graduation; the woman he would eventually marry. The Zimbabwean he never thought existed but brought to the USA for a purpose.* For a few seconds, his thoughts wondered far away only to be interrupted by another round of applause for yet another student receiving her certificate.

Big auntie could not hold back her emotions as she hugged Susan, tears rolling down her chicks. Her uncle just looked at her and muttered, "God is good, God is good". What a day.

Fareed sneaked and congratulated Susan. He didn't even hug her in front of her uncle as he was not sure of his response.

Susan: "Uncle this is Fareed, he is a good friend. We are together here at University. He is from Iraq," Susan was quick enough to slot in a short conversation. Intentional? You bet. And uncle just looked at Fareed and smiled.

Uncle: "She has done well hasn't she" uncle looked Fareed in the face forensically gauging what sort of friend he was.

Fareed: "Yes, it's wonderful. I am happy for her, Fareed responded as uncle moved on to greet another couple whom he recognised.

It was a great day and Susan could not believe this was it. Her days were numbered in the USA unless if she got a job. *She thought of what would now happen. Long stretches of work and perhaps not seeing Fareed for a long time depending on whether he would go back to join his family in Qatar. These were unknowns and she kept praying that it would work out in the end.*

Following Fareed's graduation, he flew back to the Middle

East with his parents. It was a sombre farewell when he said goodbye to Susan. They had just finished coffee at one of their favourite cafés near the University after spending an hour talking about their future and the various scenarios. It was difficult to find out how their relationship would pan out. The many unknowns regarding the attitudes of their parents and whether this was indeed God's will for their lives. Since Fareed had several friends in the USA, he knew that he would be back soon. Susan's plans were not clear. Unless she got a job in the next few months, she would have to do the inevitable and go back to her motherland. This would be a last resort as prospects of her getting a job there were non-existent. Besides, this would mean not seeing Fareed for a season.

Uncle: "So, what are your plans Susan, you know we are praying that God will give you a good job.," uncle began what would end up being a vital heart to heart conversation. They discussed all the possible scenarios. Possible job offers from where she did her internship. Suddenly her uncle remembered something.

"That friend, was it Fareed, the one you said was from Iraq. did you mean just friend or real friend?" Susan: "Uncle," Susan started giggling

Uncle: "Oh, I seem to have touched a raw nerve here judging by your facial response".

Come on what is it? Something of interest?" Uncle continued to ask.

Susan knew, he knew. It's like he had read her mind.

Sometimes it was not easy to conceal things to her uncle whom she had known and respected for years.

Susan: "Yes uncle, he is a real friend. He is my boyfriend." She started sobbing.

He knew right away that she was in love.

Uncle: "Come on Susan. God is the only one who can help and make your dreams come true. Once you two are clear about what God is saying, that is all that matters to me. whether he comes from Mars or wherever, it is your relationship that counts. If you two are happy, all we can do is to pray for you and support you in any way we can until you decide to do something more serious. Susan, he said laughing, how on earth did you find this handsome Iraqi guy. God never ceases to amaze me. I suppose those are some of the implications of living in the Diaspora. Has he told his parents?

Susan: "No uncle, he will do so when he gets to Qatar where they live and work." Susan replied, glad this had come up and that one hurdle had been overcome. If uncle was happy with it the door had now been opened. He is one of the family members who had influence. People tended to listen when he spoke. He was respected. He was a man of integrity. A load had been taken from her shoulders. Now the ball was in Fareed's court. She couldn't wait to tell him.

Staying at her uncle's place proved to be the best thing that ever happened to Susan. How long, depended on how quickly she would be offered a job. If not, she would fly out to Zimbabwe when her visa expired.

A few days after Fareed graduated, he was heading back to Qatar. He had met Susan several times and was excited when he heard of Susan's famous conversation with her uncle.

Fareed: "Susan, this is an answer to prayer. Now you can pray the same thing to happen when I break the news to my parents. Mine is a steeper mountain to climb. You know what I mean", Fareed began to talk about possible hitches but always hopeful that his dad, a former diplomat would come in handy. Besides, his mum born in the USA would be a great influence.

Fareed: "Dad has seen it all. He is used to cultural diversity, or they would not have sent him to so many countries. Do you know that at one time he did a stint in Sierra Leone!"

Susan: "Fareed – Susan assured Fareed – we have prayed and have settled this between ourselves, so we just must stay focused. Besides, it is still way away; unless you wanted to marry me tomorrow,"

Susan squeezed Fareed's palm smiling broadly. You could tell she was really in love. To her he was no Iraqi but her confidant, someone she looked forward to sharing her life with. These last few days when they found time to talk were precious. There was so much to talk about including Fareed's job offers. A Kuwait Company was interested in him, so was the company his dad worked for. One New York Oil conglomerate had written asking for his Curriculum vitae and for the possibility of him working as an intern for a year. Things were happening fast for Fareed, and he needed the wisdom to choose what to do.

Susan: "Fareed, this is good news. I am happy for you. I

can't believe, I may not see you for some time. I don't want to think about it now. I am happy we are together for now." Susan said her last words as Fareed bade farewell.

CHAPTER 22
HOME SWEET HOME

Fareed was surprised to see a whole tribe waiting for him at Doha airport. Her cousins and nieces had flown to Doha earlier from Baghdad risking their lives. It was indeed a home coming of some sort. His dad's palatial home on the outskirts of the city was stunning. Double storied with all the trappings of a home fit for a king. There was a sea of green carpeting the whole garden and shrubs vying for attention as flowers blossomed at the edge of the driveway. The desert heat and sand were driven away by the opulence of it all. Fareed had been home when his parents first moved to Qatar. But this was out of this world. And his dad's company was well known for spoiling its executives let alone CEOs of whom Fareed's dad was one.

It was past midnight when they finally retired to their bedrooms. Fareed had to make a quick call to Susan as he couldn't earlier because of all the excitement. He did not care about the five-hour difference between Doha and Cincinnati.

Fareed: "Hey Susan, "Fareed's excitement was palpable over the phone.

Susan: "Fareed, Fareed, Susan equally excited. What kept you. You got me worried. Did you arrive safely. Who was

Who will marry me?

there? Were they excited? I miss you already. I bet its boiling," Susan kept going before Fareed could slot in his side of the story. He was used to this now. When Susan was excited, no one could stop her; but it was understandable. Here she was, alone. Well not quite, she had her auntie and uncle with her but of course it was not the same.

Fareed: "Hi babe, I miss you too. Guess what? The whole tribe was at the airport. And my dad's place has been transformed. It's unbelievable. I will send you some photos in the morning. This is the home for the rich and famous. I don't think I like this. It's too much. Remember what Jesus said, 'Foxes have holes, and birds of the air have nests, but the Son of Man has nowhere to lay his head' Matthew 8:20 ESV. How are you keeping.?"

They went on and on for longer than they had anticipated. It was after 3 am when Fareed went to bed. He struggled to find some sleep as many thoughts raced through his mind. The thoughts turned into dreams until he woke up very late.

Many offers for jobs arrived for Fareed and he had to decide on which one to go for. There were two offers from the USA and the rest were in the Middle East including his dad's company. This became a subject of conversation at home. His parents were open minded but would prefer him staying in the Middle East. Uncle Ali was definite about the Middle East. His reason?

Fareed's phone kept ringing and his mum tried to ignore

173

it. She saw that it was an overseas number and decided to answer it.

Fareed's mum: "Hello, Fareed is in the kitchen. Who is it?" The person made a slight cough as if trying to clear her throat.

Susan: "Sorry I will phone later if he is busy. My name is Susan, I went to University with Fareed," Susan gathered courage. Fareed grabbed the phone from mum and ran straight to his bedroom. He appeared an hour later with a grin and a face which lit up.

Mum: "Eh Fareed, were you still talking, Mum became inquisitive. Who is this Susan son? Where is she from? Anything we must know about her? Sorry but by the look in your eyes, something tells me that she is special. We have been there too Fareed." Mum began her charming diplomatic offensive. She knew if it was serious, Fareed would eventually confide in her.

Fareed: "Mama, its nothing. She is just a friend. She is from Zimbabwe." Fareed carefully responded to his mum.

Mum: "Is this what has happened to you in the USA since you joined church? Do you know where Zimbabwe is. It's Africa, son. I hope you are not serious. It's a different world from us here. Sorry I didn't mean to intrude," mum sensitively navigated this potential mine field. *She knew she could either make or break her relationship with the only son she had.*

Fareed seemed not to care. He had rehearsed these moments many times when he was at University and here was his chance to convince mum, with God's help. He slipped into the sofa close to mum.

Fareed: Mama, I am in love with this girl. She loves me. Not only that, but she also loves Jesus. Remember when I told you what happened to me at church in the States. I have embraced the Jesus of the Bible and so has Susan. Yes, she is from Zimbabwe. She is African but that is not important to us. All that matters is that we found each other and one day we intend to marry with your support." Fareed the preacher carefully laid it out to his mum.

She just looked at him and she shed a few tears. Although she could not admit it, she was impressed with her son and how he was becoming a man. *She saw signs of maturity which the average student did not have. Whatever relationship he had with this Susan from Zimbabwe; it seems it was for real. Are* they having a mum to son talk, dad wondered as he walked into the lounge?

Dad: "What's up Fareed. You are really mama's baby." He laughed as he sat on his rocking chair. *Fareed thought, come on Fareed this is it. I hope, you can now chip in and get this news over with.* He was right.

Fareed: "Mum, Dad, I have something to tell you. His eyes lit up as he wriggled to sit properly.

Dad: "Have you had other job offers?" dad asked

Mum: "Fareed has a serious relationship with a girl from Zimbabwe" mum stepped in. Dad's eyes popped up. He poked his ears, took off his glasses and looked straight into Fahima, his wife.

Dad: "Sorry, you took me by surprise. Say that again. Mahmud pretended not to have understood what Fahima was saying.

Mum: "I am as surprised as you. It's not stale news. I have just heard this a few minutes ago. If I had not picked up Fareed's phone, I wouldn't have known. We need to find out from Fareed. I have nothing against Zimbabwe or ... I mean a people of that... Sorry. I am ok with it. What am I saying? We don't even know whether this is a serious relationship yet."

There was a moment of silence. *Was this what America had brought to their door? Could this be one of the consequences of sending their son to distant land?.*

Dad: "Fahima, Fahima, there is nothing to worry about. Remember as a diplomat I was privileged to work in many countries with diverse cultures and traditions. Do you remember our good friends from Jamaica and Senegal? Do you?" Mahmoud spoke with unconvincing courage as he tried to persuade his wife that all was well. *Encountering diversity before was different from diversity knocking on their door one day. This was the stuff that dreams were made of. But there was no running from reality. A girl called Susan from Zimbabwe, Africa, had phoned their son in Qatar, in their living room. Fahima had just answered the phone. The joy of welcoming Fareed and the great Graduation celebration paled into insignificance as they now realised the need to get real and prepare to hear it from the horse's mouth. These thoughts raced in Mahmud's mind.*

Fareed walked into a stone-cold living room. A few minutes before it was ringing with laughter and joy, now the atmosphere had completely changed.

"What's up, Fareed muttered in Arabic or the equivalent of it. He threw himself on the couch and continued eating a sandwich he had just made in the kitchen. Susan's auntie came for the graduation. All the way from Zimbabwe. I was not able to meet her. It's too early. Sorry mum and dad. Maybe I should formally let you know what has happened between me and Susan.

Dad: "Is she just a friend from University. How did you two meet? Is she engaged to someone? As you can see Fareed we just need some clarification," Dad quickly interrupted Fareed in the hope that he could confirm what he wanted to hear.

Fareed: "We are serious about our relationship. First time I met her was in the lab. It was obvious something was bound to happen. Mum and dad, I know it is difficult to imagine, but I want to marry her one day. Hopefully, it will be soon, once I get a good job and we can plan. I love her very much. I have told her about you and how you through the job you used to do, are tolerant of many cultures. Mum, I have mentioned to her that you were born in the USA. When I spoke to Uncle Ali I was afraid to tell him about her as he seemed bent on me finding an Arab girl in the USA.", Fareed paused. He needed instant assurance from his parents.

Dad: "Son, you should have told us from the beginning when you thought you were interested in this girl. We would have advised you and warned you of some of the challenges. What does her parents do for a living, for example? Would she be accepted in our community and many such issues. Anyway, that is history now. Don't get me wrong. At the end of the day, it is your decision. But you know very well that your parents' approval matters too."

Mahmoud struggled to mouth these few sentences. He was caught between culture and what he had learnt as a diplomat. He too was trained in the USA. He married a USA born wife, although of Arabic heritage. That is why he sent Fareed there. He too had had close encounters with many girls from all over the world. Fahima happened to be at the right place at the right time. That is why he ended up tying the note with her. Upon reflection he knew his son too had faced the same reality and decided otherwise.

Mum: "Fareed Fareed, thank you for letting us know. I am sure you will understand how we feel. It's not like you are married to her now. It's still a relationship in its infancy. It may come to nothing after all. Especially when you know that you may not see each other for some time. Time is a great doctor you know. It heals many things, and it clarifies many things. So, let's wait and see what is going to happen. I just can't imagine your Susan coming to live with us here. She may not like it, or her parents may stop her from coming. We are really very different cultures. Anyway, sorry that we seem to be throwing spanners into your relationship, but as your parents we are concerned. Please don't take it personally." Mum threw in the towel with her eyes fix on Fareed who was listening attentively with a certain calmness spread across his face.

They did not realise that he had rehearsed all these scenarios while he was in the USA. They had talked about this and the possible responses. This was the expected happening in his very eyes. So much prayer had gone into this, and Fareed was praying while listening to his parents.

Fareed: "Thanks mum, thanks dad. You mean a lot to me. When this all happened while I was away, I thought of you and wished you were with me to witness what God was doing in my life. I told you that I had given my life to Jesus Christ. He is no longer one of the prophets to me. He is God and he came to die for me on the cross so that I may have abundant life. I have been talking to him about my future including whom he wants me to have for a wife. I know this seems inappropriate to talk about these things when I have just graduated from College. But for some reason, God sorted this puzzle during my college years and brought Susan from Zimbabwe into my life. So, I appreciate your concerns, but I would ask that you respect my decision so far. I am hoping that Susan can come and visit sometime when she gets a job or when I do as well. You must see her. She is out of this world I promise you. When you meet her, you will not see the Zimbabwean in her, but a woman fearfully and wonderfully made."

Dad: "Alright son. You are still here with us, and we will talk about these things some other time. Thanks for letting us know. No wonder why Americans say, 'You haven't seen nothing Yet!' Dad quipped with a grin on his face.

Meanwhile, Susan was having the best time of her life with most of her relations in town. Her uncle could not hide his joy at what Susan had accomplished. Every evening during prayers he belted the song *To God be the glory* Lyrics by Frances J. Crosby. This was a miracle. No girl in their families had achieved so much. Most of them got married in their teens and were scattered all over Zimbabwe. Susan was the only one who had ventured abroad. She was the jewel in the crown. A blessing. A heritage. Everyone was proud of her. She had followed her uncle's footsteps. And he was very proud that all the immediate family was able to join him for Susan's graduation.

Susan's aunt: "Susan while I am proud of you for what you have achieved so far, there is only one thing left. If that happened, then I will be happy to say goodbye to this world. Whoever imagined I could fly as I did to see all of you here," auntie started her favourite conversation. She was brought in the tradition that believed, *until you are married, you really haven't achieved much. A girl needs a husband, a bus load of children and an atmosphere of love and joy which only a family can give.*

Susan's uncle: "Eh mama, she has to find a young man to marry first before all else", Susan's uncle interrupted as he dug deep into his plate of maize meal porridge drowned in a concoction of meat and vegetable stew. Sadza in short. It was amazing that after ten years in the United States, the Zimbabwean in him stubbornly resisted change. He hardly suffered from cultural erosion. No wonder why Susan continued this legacy.

Auntie: "How do you know that she has not found a man. You know these girls don't tell you. Her mother probably knows. Ask her," great auntie displayed a wisdom that only people of her age could exhibit. This was the beginning of an unravelling of what many never knew and only Susan had kept to herself. She had waited for this opportunity and the coming of big auntie came in handy.

Susan brought a jug of water from the kitchen for all to wash down their appetising meal. And auntie attacked immediately.

Auntie: "Susan is it true you have found a young man who wants to marry you?", auntie went on the offensive.

Susan: "Oh auntie, who told you that. "she sheepishly left the jug and dashed back to the kitchen. The dice had now been cast. There was no going back.

CHAPTER 23
THE DICE IS CAST

For both Susan and Fareed there was no escape from reality. The world was not a good place anymore and tolerance among cultures and religions was at a low ebb. Even what they considered "home" was not the same anymore. Falling in love was in a way a façade. It bloated the coarse reality under the surface. And it was the peeling of those unpalatable layers of prejudice, intolerance, and sometimes racism that meant hard work. The media was awash daily with stories of men and women wrapped in relationships that they could not sustain, not because of themselves, but because of the pressures from outside. The ability to ride rough shod against such was a triumph. And these two hoped that this would happen and vindicate the God they believed in who had said, "And surely I am with you always, to the very end of the age" Matthew 28:20(b) NIV.

There is a sense in which it was perhaps too much to expect from these two recent graduates who still had age and wisdom on their side to come out of this unscathed. Bruised they would be like many married giants before them, but they would remain standing even after the onslaught. That remained their hope. But meanwhile they were miles apart separated by both the oceans and the desert.

After submitting loads of applications, Susan started to lose hope. Time had sailed by and yet eight months down the line she was still without a job. Fortunately her visa would expire in the next year and a half. There was still time to plod on until she could secure a job. But how long would she have to wait. And more importantly how long could Fareed hang on. There were no quick fixes to life. Not many companies were recruiting lawyers because of the economic downturn in many countries. But Susan held on. At least she had a roof over here head at her uncle's place. She had quickly settled in her uncle's church and found many acquaintances who, too, were in the same predicament.

Susan: "Hi Fareed, where are you. I miss you so much," Susan burst with excitement. This was one of the weekly calls Fareed made from Doha, Qatar.

Fareed: "Sue, I am great girl. Burning in the desert here. I can't stand it. But I have good news. I am flying to New York for an interview next month. I can't believe it. It is with BP Oil. Susan I will be back in the US. Susan just went cold. *Her imagination running riot. Fareed, in the USA? For an interview? With BP oil?* Before she could answer, Fareed went on.

Fareed: "And Susan, talk to your people, I am ready to meet with your uncle. You must introduce me to him. This is our opportunity. I am sure they will offer me a job. The head of the Recruiting Division knows my dad very well and I am sure something is going to come out of it. Susan paused with excitement. She hardly had time to process her response.

Susan: "Brilliant. I will let my uncle know. I am sure it will be fine. We've got to go through this now Fareed. Next stop is your parents. Alright?" Susan spoke confidently. This was it. The process had started. They were on their way to their promised land. The wilderness desert was in front of them, but they had great confidence in the One who had brought them together.

Fareed had gone through a series of interviews before he arrived in New York. This included telephone, zoom and computer model ones.

On the day for the face-to-face interview, there were three gentlemen and two ladies in the Board room. All sat stone faced as Fareed walked in. First, he had to make a presentation on power point before they asked him mainly technical questions. They broke for lunch and when they came back, they were joined by the chief engineer of the project. He too asked a few questions. By this time, there was a certain cordiality in the air. Fareed was asked to complete a few forms and told that the HR department would contact him in a week.

Susan had to let her uncle know that Fareed was in town. Fortunately, she had mentioned about him before and he seemed to be liberal about him.

Susan: "Uncle do you remember my friend Fareed that I talked to you about.",

Uncle: "The guy from Iraq?" Uncle replied

Susan: "Yes but he is now living in Qatar. it's the same Middle East."

Uncle: "What about him"? uncle asked rather surprised

Susan: "He is back in the USA. He came for a job interview in New York. I would like to introduce him to you and everyone. Is that ok uncle? If he came say next Thursday, just for an hour or so." This seemed abrupt. Uncle had still not mentioned to the untie who came for graduation. But for him it didn't matter.

Uncle: "That's fine let's get it over with. Let him come. I will see what I can do and let your mum and dad know and of course auntie. I can't believe we are about to receive a guy from Iraq, an Arab guy in our family. But that is how God works. He has a great sense of humour."

Fareed stayed with some of his friends in New York after the interview. He could not believe that they both had fast tracked the process. He was not just here for the job interview but for the mother of all interviews that is, access to Susan's family.

Susan's parents did not see this coming. They had come for their daughter's graduation, but now she was about to announce something they never imagined; a serious friendship with someone of another tribe and race. A foreigner in their view. It was difficult to get this across to uncle. He had been a pillar in their family and over the years gained a lot of respect.

"Uncle, where did you say this boy comes from? they asked in unison

"Iraq. He is Arabic from the Middle East.", uncle began

to explain to Susan's parents what she had confided in him. Everything; Fareed's character, how they met and how much he was in love with Jesus Christ.

It was agreed that Fareed would only meet Susan's uncle and his wife. It was too early for him to meet Susan's parents as this was contrary to tradition. So, there was no fanfare on the day. He got a taxi and was met by Susan who escorted him home to the small semi-detached house at the end of a terraced complex. When they got to the lounge, uncle and auntie were seeping some tea. It proved to be one of Fareed's best days. He was relaxed and many times laughed off the uncle's joke. It was like he had come home.

"Fareed, we are happy to see and from what Susan has already told us about you, I am sure God will lead you to great things. What really impressed me was the fact that you both have a relationship with Jesus. That is a plus for you," uncle went on excitedly. By the time Fareed left, he too felt like this was a visit planned in heaven. But uncle gave Fareed and Susan a word of caution. Not everyone was going to view their relationship kindly. They must prepare for the worst, but God would help them, and he was there to assist wherever he could.

Fareed landed the job with BP Oil. His parents were rather disappointed as they preferred him working in Qatar. But it was not to be. For Fareed this was an opportunity to be near Susan at a time they were now serious about marriage. There was so much to prepare before he moved to the USA. Fortunately, the company offered executive accommodation for its engineers especially those still starting off. He secured accommodation on 65ᵗʰ Avenue. He would travel on the Metro and on to the Company bus. These were exciting times and Fareed could not wait. This was the beginning of a career.

Since Fareed was the only son, his parents decided to fly to New York to set him up in his new flat. They would stay in the Marriott Hotel while they were there. This was welcome news and Fareed broke this news to Susan:

Fareed: "Susan my parents are coming with me to New York. I was wondering if I could introduce you to them while they are there? She was surprised. Meeting Fareed's parents?

Susan: "Oh, well, I don't know whether I am ready and still can't believe I am actually meeting them?

Fareed: "Stop it Susan, remember when you asked me to meet your uncle during my interview?"

Susan: "Alright, I was just kidding. Let me know when so I can decide when to let uncle and auntie know. Fareed, it's all happening. I can't believe it. God is good," Susan spoke with tears on her cheeks. *This was overwhelming. She always thought of her upbringing, what had happened since and how she was on the verge of a relationship that would show God's favour on her life.*

CHAPTER 24
THE GREAT ENCOUNTER

As they flew above the high rise buildings over the New York skyline, Fareed could clearly see the statue of Liberty on Manhattan island. The plane hovered in circles waiting for permission to land at LaGuardia airport. His parents travelled executive class, courtesy of their company. As the Airbus 787 touched the tarmac, it was welcome to the Big Apple for Fareed.

They checked in to the Marriot hotel where Fareed would stay for the night before heading to his new apartment. The beginning of a new life of work and adulthood.

Fareed's company offices were on the forty sixth floor. And it took him the whole morning sorting out work arrangements before he grabbed the keys to his new place. His parents were waiting in the lobby and together they headed for the apartment.

Fareed'"It looks impressive from outside," Fareed's mum spoke encouragingly to her only son.

The place looked clean and seemed someone had been inside to give it a spring clean. There was a corridor interleading to other apartments. A reasonable sized bedroom, kitchen and a smallish lounge with leather sofas that had had their day. The view outside was stunning. It overlooked the Hudson river with boats crossing from the harbour to the island.

Fareed: "Dad, look, Fareed spoke in Arabic. This is great. I like the scenery from here.

They both sat on the couch and there was a sense of satisfaction from both parents as they began to imagine life without their son. This was it. Almost the end of their Project Children. All that was left was for Fareed to talk about his impending manhood and announce that someone had come into his life.

Dad: "Look after this apartment son. You need to show them that you are responsible. I know you are," Mahmud spoke proudly of his son. He had been a good model. And his career as a diplomat was evidence of this.

Fareed: "Thanks mum and dad for coming and being with me while I settle. Unfortunately, you will have to continue staying in your hotel as you can see that there is no space for all of us, "Fareed giggled as he spoke.

Fareed had to get the basics for his apartment and before long it looked habitable. It took just a day or two. His mum worked hard going to and from the hotel and making sure that their son was comfortable.

Dad: "We are flying back next week, and I am sure you will find this place great. Enjoy your work Fareed and never stop working hard. It is all about excellence. That is what builds your character and gives you a good reputation," dad spoke slowly, knowing that these could be his last words before his son dived into the jungle which is the world of today.

Fareed: "Excuse me", Fareed sneaked into the kitchen to answer the phone.

It was Susan. They spoke endlessly.

Fareed: "Alright Susan I will say a word to my parents as long as you are sure you will be here on Wednesday. My dad is very particular about time keeping," Fareed spoke saying his goodbye.

Fareed: Dad: "Sorry, that was Susan."

Dad: "You mean the girl who phoned you in Doha?" dad replied.

Fareed: "Yes, she is in Florida. Her uncle lives there, and both her Mum, Dad and great auntie came for the Graduation from Zimbabwe." *Fareed knew this was his opportunity to break the ice.* Remember I said that I was serious about this girl. I meant it. Since you are here, I would like Susan to come next Wednesday before you fly out. This is a great opportunity for you to meet her. Is that, ok?

This was like a lightning bolt. Unexpected. Both were ill prepared for it. Fareed gave them no choice. Dad: "What will we say to her", dad retorted. Are you that serious"?

Mum: "He must be, let's give him the benefit of the doubt. We shall see her when she comes." Mum gave a definitive response". Once the matter was settled, Fareed relayed the news to Susan. There was no time to waste.

Susan was elegant in stature, very beautiful. She had a presence whenever she walked in a place. and her smile could easily dislodge any fits of anger. She was just likeable. And her faith in Jesus seemed to have made her face light up with joy. As she walked into the apartment escorted by Fareed, there was an eerie silence. Fareed's parents looked and before Fareed could introduce her, Fahima his mum stood up and embraced Susan kissing her in true Middle east style. Susan ran cold.

Susan: "Good to see you mama," the words just popped from Susan's mouth. Fahima looked Susan in the eyes and uncharacteristically and without thinking uttered her response.

"Welcome home. Thank you."

By the time Mahmud stood up to greet Susan, Fahima had stolen the thunder. She had broken the ice and the environment was already conducive.

Mahmud: "Hello, good to see you, sit down," Mahmud spoke gently and unemotionally.

They settled down. Fareed made some tea and cake and they spoke for ages. The conversation was more of an interrogation than a normal conversation. But it was worth it. Fareed was mesmerised. He could not believe what he was witnessing. *Surely God answers prayer, he thought.* Susan became part of the family straight away.

They arranged to see Susan's uncle and her parents before they flew out to Qatar. Susan and Fareed's journey had begun. It was not a fairy tale anymore. God had granted their request and cultural diversity was no longer a barrier for now. There was a template many young men and women from different cultures and traditions could use. This was indeed a story to tell for the rest of their lives.

Meanwhile Susan as soon as she got back to her uncle, she had work to do to convince her mum and dad of the importance of meeting Fareed's parents while they were still in the USA.

Susan's Mum: "If you want to involve us you've got to go by the book. If you were in Zimbabwe, would you have gone and met Fareed's parents?", Susan's mum spoke rather cross that should her father hear about this, the intended visit of Fareed's parents would be aborted.

Susan: "Sorry mum but I was well received. They are the nicest people I have ever met. You must have been there to appreciate it. I could sense in my spirit that this relationship was of God's choosing." Susan carefully tried to convince mum

Susan's mum tended to shoot from the hip a bit. However inwardly she approved of her daughter's courage and tenacity. She had heard a lot from the uncle to appreciate what Fareed and Susan were up to. Susan's mum was determined to convince her husband and win him over before Mahmud and Fahima came over.

CHAPTER 25
THE FAMILIES MEET

Uncle's house was a far cry from the posh mansion that was Fareed's parents in Doha. And yet there was a certain ambience and warmth in the place. It was like a reservoir in the desert where peace and serenity were in abundance. The sort of place where one could often come in an emergency to seek shelter and comfort. This day was no different. Fareed had been grilled about Zimbabwean cultural protocols before he escorted his parents into the house. Susan used to make fun of Fareed when he gave them lessons in the appropriate handclapping and demeanour as any would be in law approached his mother and father-in-law. He was not there yet but that respect had to be demonstrated as a way of wooing them to his side.

Mahmoud and Fahima had a two-day course with Fareed. It didn't matter much but at least it was important that they knew. As a former diplomat, Fareed's dad was aware of this.

Fareed led the way into the small lounge where everyone was sitting. Uncle stood up and came to greet Fareed.

Uncle: "Welcome, welcome. Hello, welcome," the eccentric uncle went on.

Susan, who was in the kitchen, came straight in but could

not hide her joy. She plunged into Fahima's arms and politely greeted Mahmud. Her mum and dad and auntie remained fixed on the sofa. They resisted getting excited and wanted to show everyone that there was a Zimbabwean culture to protect no matter who was in the house. There was silence and uncle then stood up and started doing the introductions. Big auntie as soon as she saw Fareed could not help ululating. She wanted to relish every moment.

Uncle: "Thank you, Jesus, thank you Jesus- uncle responded-. Our children thought that we should know each other. This is an informal gathering but because Fareed's parents were in this country, they thought they would come and see you." uncle slowly navigated the murky cultural waters.

Uncle was very careful not to give the impression that this was the real thing. This was the starter before the main course and the children were keen to have their families with them from the start of their journey. There was an invisible bond even during this short visit between the two families. For a moment all the doubts about race, religion and culture seemed to vanish. The main actors were their children and what was best for them. They were the actors on the stage, and what a beginning!

Following the rollercoaster visits by Fareed and Susan to their respective parents, one would have thought that this was it and there were no more mountains to climb. Or were there? Susan was very fortunate to land a job in sunny California just outside LA. It was a small firm of solicitors specialising in both

Commercial Law and Immigration issues. It was a very busy office for its size. People from Mexico, Afghanistan, Africa, and even Fiji and the Solomon Islands came to seek legal advice, desperate to enter the land of opportunity. Susan blended well and slowly began to enjoy her work. Unfortunately, because she had only just joined the firm, she was not able to bid farewell to her mum and dad and auntie following their six months stint following her graduation. This was no big deal as she had achieved her major dream of arranging the meeting of the two families. This was huge. They represented the tribe back home and would be able to tell the story.

Susan: 'Hello mum, Sorry I can't be at the airport, but I hope you will have a safe flight. Be careful at Dubai airport. You have a long wait but make sure you keep looking at the flight board. Uncle George was stranded there a few years ago after he missed his flight.'

Mum: 'We will be careful. You know your dad is very particular about these things. Take care of yourself and take time to know Fareed. Please continue to find out about him from his friends. These cultural issues are very real you know. Sorry I don't mean to upset you. He is a fine young man I know." Mum spoke like she would never see her daughter again but as a mum she was not sure about Fareed and Susan together. *She just hoped and prayed that all would go well. She thought of Fareed's parents, how posh they looked and yet humble. How would her daughter fit in let alone their relatives?*

The first few weeks were difficult for Fareed. He worked like an intern and there was so much to learn about chemical engineering at the plant. While what he learnt at university was useful, the application of some of the concepts became harder and harder. Fortunately, he was paired with a very skilled gentleman from Oklahoma. He had been in the industry for many years, although he had only done an engineering diploma after college, he had so much experience over the years that many undergraduates at the company had passed through his hands. His name was Killian, but they called him "King".

Killian: "So, you say your dad works in Qatar. Why did he leave the diplomatic field with all the travelling and perks? I guess he is earning more money where he is", King kept probing each time he had coffee breaks with Fareed.

He was American to the core and his knowledge of the world ended in the Hudson River. He could hardly pronounce Qatar let alone other countries in the world. Fareed did not mind. His concern was how he could influence King to appreciate what Jesus Christ had done for him and the rest of the world. Fareed never lost his faith. He stuck to his guns when it came to what he believed. And many at the company could see the difference in the young man who had joined the company.

"Fareed, do you have a girl, or you dumped her when you left university," King began the long process of scrutinising Fareed's personal life,

Fareed: "Oh yea, she is in LA. We are so much in love."

Killian: "Is she from your part of the world? I bet she is American. Many of you lot seem to want American gals, eh" King retorted with a smile.

Fareed: "She is from Zimbabwe. Have you heard of Zimbabwe?"

Killian: "You are kidding. You mean in Africa. What? I don't understand you guys sometimes. I don't mean to be rude, but they are different you know. What will your parents say about it? An Afro American would have been much better."

Fareed knew that people held such views, but this was the first time to come face to face with a potential racist but he kept his cool.

Fareed: "My parents met her when they came for the Graduation, and I also met her parents. So, it's all sorted out King don't worry.

Killian: "Sorry for being a bit intrusive," Killian apologised.

Fareed: "That's ok. You know what binds me and my girlfriend together more than anything else? We love the Lord Jesus. So, it's kind of fun.

This stunned King as he changed the subject. Fareed was aware that this was the beginning of many interrogations that would come regarding his relationship with Sue. But he was happy that there were so many in the USA who were in a similar predicament. The crunch was to be able to respond appropriately each time this subject came up. He also began to imagine what his Arab friends and relatives were going to say.

Every night Fareed and Susan would talk over the phone. There was so much to share regarding their hurts, stresses at work and the issues concerning their relationship highlighted by friends and colleagues.

On Susan's side her newly found friends wanted her to

appear inferior being in love with a lad who came from a very rich family. All that did not deter her and in fact emboldened her together with her faith in Jesus Christ. She occasionally spoke to her best friend Melissa in the UK who too had challenges in her relationship with Keith. Not between themselves but from outside forces who sought to put spanners in their relationship.

As they shared with Susan, they encouraged each other. Melissa was looking forward to Susan's wedding one day. Though this was still premature, yet they already discussed possible venues, bridesmaids and all the trappings of a great marriage. In fact their dreams had come true. Well, almost as they never thought of having relationships with men from other cultures. But this was what the diaspora brought to their lives. They now had to reconfigure their faith, attitudes, in the light of their newly found environment.

In both Qatar and Zimbabwe, two families had time to chew the cud after their visit to their children's graduation. It was time to look back and consider what they had done. They had inadvertently endorsed their sibling's relationship. They had not been given a chance to consult those at home. There was no time. The dice had been cast and what will be will be.

Mahmoud: "Fahima, do you know what we have done. We have in a way welcomed Susan into our family. I must say that girl has something I can't pinpoint. She is special. She is from Zimbabwe, but oh what a lady." Mahmoud confessed his satisfaction at what he felt meeting his son's girlfriend. He was bowled over. There was no doubt in his mind that she would make a special daughter in law.

Fahima: "Well, well, you seem to have been impressed Mahmoud. She is not Arab you know. Are you forgetting that", Fahima started teasing her husband who, like Uncle Ali was always keen on beautiful Arab girls from the Middle East?

Mahmoud: "Sorry, but I agree with you. Did you see me that day when she walked into Fareed's apartment? There was something in that girl like a magnet which just swayed me. Could it be this Jesus Fareed always talks about? I agree with you, all I could see was a friend. Someone that I can confide in and who would be a great wife for our son," Mahmoud agreed

Fahima fell back into the sofa wondering what all this was about. She began to understand what the decision to send their son to university away from home entailed. A simple decision for the sake of their son was beginning to affect his destiny. Many of their friends had left their homeland for other distant lands. It wasn't just Iraqis but Europeans and Africans like Susan. And many families had been split for better or for worse. This was the new norm. sometimes dictated by the need to create wealth for their families. And for others it was for mere survival. The stark choice was that either you stay in your home country and face possible death, torture, or some other calamity that mother nature brought one's way. It was complex but many had to navigate through such complexities to make ends meet. Suddenly the world was a new place; and for many there was no preparatory school for it.

All this occupied Mahmoud and Fahima. Every day they

would wonder what the future held for their son and the inevitable daughter in law to be, Susan. They now had little influence. New York and Doha were miles apart. Social media was no substitute for face-to-face encounter with their son. Their prayer was that whatever they had instilled in their son would stick and become handy as he ploughed through the highs and lows of his relationship. They were confident that Fareed's newfound faith would be enough to steer him towards the shore of marriage. Besides, Susan was equally in the same boat and her African upbringing would be something that will augur well on the journey.

CHAPTER 26
NEAR-MIS

After seven months of being apart and relying on social media to catch up, Fareed had had enough. It took some time for Susan to answer the phone as she was stuck in a conversation on the landline with Melissa in the UK. They had so much to talk about. Melissa was now on the verge of falling from the cliff age. The wedding plans were at an advanced stage and soon she would become Mrs Keith Parsons of Oxford.

Susan: "Melissa, hold on. I think Fareed is phoning on my work mobile", Susan giggled as she ran to answer.

Susan: "Hi, love, sorry Melissa is on the line, but I will just say goodbye and phone you", She was so excited. Fareed on one hand and Melissa on the other. Only one conversation about love.

Susan: "Bye Melissa. I will phone you. Baba(daddy)is on the phone. I can't believe I am saying this."

Melissa: "Ok bye Susan", Melissa hung up. Fareed's phone started ringing again and they talked and talked as they usually did.

Fareed: "I will fly to LA on Saturday next week and fly

back Sunday. There is a B&B near your place just for the night," the plan was already on the table.

Susan: "That will be fine Fareed. I am looking forward to it. Did I tell you that mum and dad and auntie are now flying back to Zimbabwe next month? They seem very happy. I am surprised at the way they took our relationship. They are excited Fareed. Can you believe that?

Fareed: "Yes, I can, -Fareed started giggling- I am just what they ordered, a handsome young Arab gentleman!" Susan just laughed her heart out.

When he arrived in LA, Fareed took an Uber taxi to the B& B and then to Susan's apartment. It was not as spacious as Fareed's, but the decorum had a lady's touch. They spent the afternoon going through what had happened and praying for their relationship. They knew that there would be hurdles along the way but were confident that they would see them through. They spent the evening at Rossoblu one of the trendiest Italian restaurants on San Julian Street in downtown Los Angeles. This was the restaurant where the best meals are served to your satisfaction.

Susan looked elegantly tempting. She strode like a gazelle into the restaurant attracting a few blokes who were already eating away with their partners. Fareed was his normal self casual but smart. They took time to order, interrupted by tons of unfinished business from a few months ago. It was after ten past ten when they got a taxi to drop Susan to her apartment. Fareed was not staying long. He stood to say goodbye. Their normal hug descended into something they had never experienced before. Susan quickly realised what was about to happen.

Susan: "Shall we pray before you go?" she said in a soft inaudible tone. Fareed froze

Fareed: "Thanks Susan. I thought so too,"

He was lying. Susan had rescued him or is it God. There was an eerie silence as they thought what to say to the Jesus, they had found so dear in their lives. Pray they did and Fareed said goodbye. His short ride in the Uber taxi to his B&B was the longest five miles he had travelled. He fell flat on the single bed and thanked God for rescuing him from the abyss. They had always prayed that Jesus would not lead them into temptation. Today was a wakeup call. From now on there was need for vigilance on this long and winding road to marriage one day.

As soon as Fareed got to the airport he rang Susan to bid her goodbye after a short visit which was well worth it.

Fareed: "Susan, I am at the airport" - Fareed had now gathered his courage from yesterday's near miss Thanks Susan. You are a star. I thank God for you."

Susan "Eh Fareed, my preacher man we all need each other. Thanks for coming to see me. It's my turn now. I will be rushing to church in an hour. Pity you couldn't join me.

Fareed: "I will be in time for our evening service tonight", Fareed said as he bade farewell to Susan.

The church Susan attended was as diverse as her previous one at university. Many of the young men and women were Afro -American brothers and siters from the Hood. You couldn't tell if they came from Senegal or Zimbabwe until they opened their mouths. They loved Jesus alright, but they were different. A few Africans who were there had been in the US for ages. They came with their parents who had since left.

The brothers in the church were forthcoming. Some of them were "looking" for sisters to hook up with in the Kingdom. They sought bosom friends who would walk the journey of love with them. There was no doubt the pressure was on. It was unrelenting.

Jason Stammers and his wife Lily had been with the church for five years. It was their job as pastors to steer the ship with all the diverse teens adults, the not so young, academics and corporate executives. It was a mixture of all sorts and for a young pastoral couple it proved a big challenge. The church was fortunate to have seasoned leaders who were able to somehow meet some of the needs of this diverse congregation. They had vibrant house groups where various issues were discussed to apply the Christian faith today. And Marriage relationships was the top of the agenda for most groups.

As Susan sat in church during praise and worship, *she imagined Fareed on the plane and for a moment her mind wondered and revisited what had happened the previous night. She quickly came back to her senses and joined in the sing- a- long of her favourite tunes. Her search for a partner had now ended. Fareed was her final answer.* She sympathised with the many brothers still looking. After church, as she opened her car door, she heard someone calling her. It was Desmond. He had a heart of gold. He was known for his commitment to the cause of Christ.

Desmond: "How are you sister? I am not sure we have met. You are new to the church, alright?", he almost shouted with a smile on his face. He drove a small ford car a very rare model in the USA. He ran towards Susan.

Susan: "Hello, I am Susan. Yes, I have been coming here for the last three months."

Desmond: "I thought so. Anyway, good to meet you. I am Desmond. I work for the LA Times downtown. I did journalism as my major and I am still learning the tricks of the trade. Sorry to keep you." Desmond seemed keen to expose his resume.

Susan: "It's alright. I came to LA a few months ago. I am with Slaughter and May, the Attorneys. This was a short encounter and for Desmond it was enough as an introduction. His girlfriend was killed in a car accident two years before and this left him spiritually paralysed. He loved her and was now very careful about new relationships.

Desmond: "Sorry Susan to hold you. You are welcome here. I hope you will like it. See you later,"

Desmond quickly ran back to his car. Susan slowly left the car park. Sunday afternoons were very quiet for Susan. She had few friends in LA and she spent most of the time with either Fareed or Melissa on the phone. As soon as Susan got home she called Melissa.

Susan: "Melissa how are you."

Melissa: Hi Sue.

Susan: I am sorry I had to cut you off on the phone the

other day. You know when he calls, everything is suspended. "She giggled as she continued from where she had left.

There was so much to talk about. Melissa and Keith's relationship had matured. They were on the verge of going over the precipice. Simply put, getting married. The man from posh Oxford was head over hills in love. She shared with Susan some of her struggles trying to win her relations to her side. This at times was an uphill battle.

For example, Melissa's auntie on her mum's side, had been in the UK for years. She worked as a nurse but remained steeped in African culture and customs. She had a natural hate for white people because of what she suffered during the war of Liberation in Zimbabwe. She sneered at anything resembling white culture. She was a Christian and very much involved in her church; but she was a great pretender. Hypocrite is the right term. She had mastered the art of plastic smiling while being lethal inside. Melissa' mum kept Melissa's relationship with Keith a secret until the last minute. That was a grave mistake.

One afternoon Keith and Melissa were visiting Melissa's parents. These visits had become regular as wedding plans were now in motion. Keith was not your typical son-in- law to be. For some reason, TK had embraced him in a way that no one could explain. Even his wife was very surprised.

Melissa's Mum: "Auntie is popping in shortly Melissa. Be prepared. I thought I was going to talk to her alone and let her know what is happening. Anyway, let it be," Melissa's mum tried to console herself. She knew what could potentially happen when the "comrade" came home. She knew she was on the firing line. As for Keith, there was nothing he could do. They had rehearsed this scenario for many months, and this was one of the implications of their decision.

Auntie: "Knock, knock," auntie bulldozed in as if to show that this was her home and all that happened in it. Keith and Melissa were in the kitchen making some tea and sandwiches. TK had just flushed the toilet and was on his way done.

Mum: "Hi sister, how are you", Melissa's mum spoke with a huge smile hiding her trepidation and uncertainty.

Mum: "Melissa, your auntie is here",

Melissa: "Oh, is she here, I thought she was in Luton. Coming".

As she opened the lounge door, Keith was close behind her. Auntie nearly choked. She did not expect this entourage. *A white man following Melissa. What was happening here, she thought.*

Melissa: "Hi auntie, This is Keith my boyfriend.". Auntie froze for a minute. She looked at TK who had just walked in, stared at Keith, who had already stretched his hand to greet her.

Keith: "Hello, I am Keith.

TK: "Oh, auntie you are here", TK pretended to be surprised. How are you." Melissa and Keith both sat down, now waiting to hear the famous response from auntie.

Auntie: "I am not staying long. I have a night shift today.

Melissa: "I will make you a cup of tea, auntie," Melissa extended her offer meant to neutralise whatever verbal venom was to come from auntie.

Auntie: `2"Stop it people". What is happening? Wo is this

man, pointing at Keith. TK knew that unless he intervened this would go out of hand.

"Auntie, he is your future son in law. Keith this is your auntie, my wife's sister. She is a nurse. Keith is a solicitor. They are planning to marry, and we are happy with it. Sorry we delayed telling you but it's a good job you came. Auntie took her sister aside and wondered why they had accepted a white man in their family. Keith easily read the situation and knew straight away that these were the signs of what was to come and what he and Melissa could expect in the long term. But they were determined to ride this wave again for the sake of their relationship. Probably the worst had just happened. Who knows?

"You know my views about these relationships" auntie finally spoke. I have nothing against you Keith, but I just think that these relationships are unsustainable. There will be so much opposition from our side as it is from your side. Our two cultures are different. Don't pretend everything is rosy. It's not. Even the Jews and Samaritans were not friends. And Jesus talked about it. I can't dictate to you what you should do but I am just warning you guys. It's not my cup of tea. Sorry if I sound negative. I am being realistic. It's just some advice. Take it or leave it."

Melissa knew that at one point this would come but not today. Her auntie was so adamant. But it was too late. The God they believed in had okayed it and they were on their way towards marriage. Unfortunately, auntie's track record was not impressive. She had had two collapsed marriages. She was never one to listen to in terms of honesty and integrity. Her hate for the other races had become an obsession but it still was disruptive and sowed seeds of doubt and uncertainty. Would it work with the new couple to be? Perhaps not. They could see through her criticism that it was hollow and was destructive and did not seek to build their relationship.

"Mary, Mary, Mary, not now please, remember these are adults and they are allowed to make their decision. We are not in the sticks in days gone by when we were at the behest of our uncles and great nieces. Besides, they seem to be serious with their faith. So please give them a break." TK quietly offered his advice while shooting from the hip a bit. This was no place for confrontations. He was aware that Keith and Melissa were pretending to make more sandwiches in the kitchen.

"TK you know me. I don't mince my words. I am not saying I am perfect but there are so many stories of young men and women who took the plunge without thinking and look where they are. Even Rev Banda's daughter did the same and now she is stuck with coloured kids in a Council flat. Is that what you want to happen to Melissa? The thing is, they will realise their mistake after it has happened. "Where is he from anyway. Do his parents and folk approve of this," Mary went on to relieve the pressure. She knew that this was a fait accompli. She may have been a bit late in the race and the wheels would not turn back, but it was worth trying."

"Why don't you ask them Mary," -her sister interrupted-softly. They are in the kitchen. You need to hear from the horse's mouth. Melissa, please come over your auntie wants to say goodbye. It was a lie. This was an invitation to the two to give their side of the story. If there was anyone in the UK who was supposed to be privy to such discussions, it was auntie Mary.

Keith and Melissa slid into the double sofa like two kids from nursery school. They were giggling inside because they had heard all and had come prepared to defend their cause. This was it. After this, they could not think of any real obstacles on Melissa's side.

"What's this I hear that you want to get married? How did it happen? Are you sure if this is right for you? Keith where do you come from. I mean in the UK. Did she tell you we are from Zimbabwe? You know where Robert Mugabe comes from, where Ian Smith colonised us?

She knew her questions were loaded with sarcasm and irony. She just wanted to scare the two.

"Aunty, sorry we did not tell you in time. I can understand your frustrations. Melissa started her defence like the solicitor she was. Keith, this is my mum's sister. She has been in this country for a long time, and she was responsible for mum coming here.", she began to introduce her fiancée cleverly.

Keith smiled and courteously said, "Nice to meet you, mainini (Auntie). He had learned this from Melissa a while back and he thought it appropriate to throw a language twist in the mix.

"What, did you say mainini?" Mary glowed with surprise. She was taken aback. Here was this white man supposedly in love with her sister's daughter appropriately addressing her. This immediately seemed to unlock everything.

"Oh, so where do you come from mwana wangu (my son)" she continued hoping that Keith would release more of his Shona vocabulary.

"My dad lives in Oxford. That is where I was born, but mum died some years ago.," Keith tore at Mary's sympathetic heart. She too had lost her mum while in the UK and was unable to attend her funeral because she was still under asylum Immigration conditions. Already, Mary began to view Keith in a different light. They were both motherless and that was something dear they had in common.

Oh, I am sorry about your mother. I lost my mum not so long ago. How is your dad. Who lives with him? she began to ask poignant questions dressed in sympathy. I hear you two are serious. I am a full member of the Methodist church you know. I hope and pray that all will go well with you. Be careful because there are many jealous people out there. We want you to do the right thing. And I am sure your mum will be happy wherever she is." Auntie Mary began to take her role as advisor. She was now the counsellor. No one had predicted this. Even TK could just look and listen in amazement at the sudden turn of events.

Mary's whistle stop tour turned to two hours of real and sensible conversation.

"What time is it? I must rush; I am doing night shifts this week and today is the first one. Nice meeting you Keith. Look after my baby. If I hear anything to the contrary, I will give you a smacking," She laughed as she exited through the back door to her car.

"Bye auntie, Mary," everyone said something.

Melissa's mum fell into her chair smiling.

"Thank you, Keith, for taking the interrogation so well. My sister has a big heart, and I am sure she was impressed. Keith just smiled and said thank you to Melissa's mum. It was ten past ten when Keith left.

There were only eleven months before the big day for Keith and Melissa. This followed a few years of preparation. There were "experts" on Keith's side of the family. People who wanted to make his wedding a model to any mixed couples who were going to marry in the future. His auntie in California had already tried to talk to Oprah Winfrey so she could influence the media to be at the wedding. It was that serious and with each passing day, new strategies were developed to make this the best wedding ever. For Melissa's mum, the wedding dress was all that occupied here and what sort of hat would match the rest of her attire. Few people would travel from Zimbabwe. Most of their relatives were already in the UK, making the family adequately represented. Keith's auntie in Australia had already made her booking to travel three months before the wedding. Her whole family was joining her. In Oxford at the Cathedral, word was buzzing that Keith was getting married. There was indeed excitement in the air among the legal fraternity on both Keith and Melissa's side. This couple was different. They were peculiar because of their faith which they stuck to all the years of their courtship. They had sailed through enormous racist and prejudice storms both at work and in their social life. It was evident from the way they conducted themselves that they were cut from a different cloth. Only time would tell what post wedding life would be like. Few people doubted their tenacity and resilience. They were a role model to many. Only one person needed to hear this good news. Susan. While they had spoken many times over the telephone, she needed to know the finality of the wedding preparations. She too had taken the same route as Susan and was building her portfolio with her great friend Fareed. This was indeed a tale of two relationships across the Atlantic.

Fareed landed at John FK around 06:30 due to a delay from LA. He knew he had already missed the evening service and would now be stuck in his apartment until the morning. There had been a few missed calls on his mobile including two from his dad in Qatar.

Fareed was keen to hear from his parents. "Hey Fareed, we tried to phone". I saw the missed call when I got off the plane. "Where were you coming from", dad was anxious?

"Oh, I thought I told you, I went to visit Susan in LA. We had a nice time. She seems to have settled well." Dad put the phone on loud so mum could hear this.

"Fareed" my son. Fahima chipped in

"Hello mum", Fareed greeted his mum

How is work" Fareed?

"It's ok. I have made a few friends. There is this older guy who thinks that I am out of my mind to have a black girl,

especially someone from Africa. He is really strange I guess."
Fareed continued.

He seemed to read his mum's mind. While she was
impressed with Susan when they last met, she had spoken to
some of her friends in Doha and those in Basra. There was a
lot of scepticism. They cautioned her into accepting such a
situation in case there was hostility from both sides afterwards.
They warned her of many young men who had tried it and
failed at the last minute. They were not able to sustain such
relationships. How could they when the cultures and the
language were completely different.

"Fareed, when are you coming home. Don't you have some
days off so we can be together, she was keen to know as this
would present an opportunity for a one to one with her.

Each time Fareed heard from his mum he expected to hear
of Uncle Ali's reaction. He was adamant that he should get a
beautiful Arab girl. To uncle Ali this was a given. He expected
Fareed's crush to be with some Asian student at the University
or something similar. There was no doubt in his mind his
sister's boy was intelligent enough to make the right decision.

"Fareed- his mum went on- the reason I was asking is that
Uncle Ali is visiting soon, and he is very keen to have a man
to man talk with you."

"I don't have leave days yet as I am still on probation.
You know with our profession we work very long hours, and
someone must be available to cover you, should you want to
take an emergency leave. I am sure I will visit soon. Give uncle
my regards when he visits. I will give him a tinkle one of these

days." Fareed was very fond of his mum and their calls were longer than usual. She was the only one who could penetrate his psyche which is why his morale was boosted after her encounter with Susan. If she approved the relationship, that was good enough for him.

Flights from Basra, had to go via Baghdad and on to Doha. Uncle Ali was very anxious as this was the first time he was flying following the protracted war. There were still pockets of resistance and security at the airport was very tight. As the plane taxied on the runway preparing for take-off, Ali had mixed feelings about making this trip in the first place. What if someone had placed a bomb on the runway or there was someone in the plane up to some mischief. It was too late, he realised. Whatever will be will be. The seat belt sign was switched off and Ali realised that they were safe in enough. It took four hours to Doha.

"Salaam. How was your flight uncle", Fareed's dad welcomed Ali as they walked towards the car? It was a short drive to where they lived. Fahima was at the door to welcome her brother whom she had not seen for some time. It was a reunion of some sort and very soon Ali was relaxed in her sister's house

. "This is a mansion" Mahmoud. You are living like you are still a diplomat. Some people are fortunate eh," Ali began rumbling on as usual. Old habits die hard. By the time they went to bed it was late in the night. Ali's was a short visit and he wanted to make the most of it. They drove him around the city graced with its palm trees and posh cars. The heat was the same as in Basra but there was an air of peace and freedom everywhere.

Friday afternoon evenings were always relaxed following prayers at the mosque. Ali never missed this.

"Do you want some strong coffee uncle". His coffee was served in a very tiny cup but brewed the Middle eastern way. He took a sip and from his facial expression you could tell that the brew was just right.

"Mahmoud, how is Fareed? You know I had a quick chat with him when he was still at university. Has he got a girlfriend now? Last time we spoke he seemed to dodge the question. And what is this I hear about him being a Christian of some sort.," Ali was genuinely keen to follow events in the life of his sister's son.

"Didn't we tell you? When we went for his Graduation, we met his girlfriend for the first time. A real surprise for us" Fahima began the careful response to Ali's questions.

"Is she from the Middle East? I am sure she is? Are there many Iraqi girls in the USA? Not that I mind. All I am interested in is a beautiful Arab girl", Uncle Ali prayed for confirmation.

"Well, Mahmoud intervened as if to rescue his wife. She is black like Somalia or Dubai girls

"Oh but is she Arab?" Uncle went on

"Not really she is from Africa. You have heard of Zimbabwe. You know where Robert Mugabe lives. She is a very nice girl. We were very impressed with her although it was for a short time. In fact, we met her parents in Florida, who had also come for her graduation. I am sure you will meet her someday uncle.

They seem serious about their relationship. Ali tried very hard to conceal his misgivings. This was not what he expected. He did not want to disappoint his sister since she seemed pleased with the girl.

"Have you spoken to Fareed. Do you know what this means to the family? What sort of baby will they have should they get married? I must speak to Fareed. I am his uncle, and I am the one to help him. Don't be fooled by what these children call love. It is a disaster. Does she speak Arabic?" Ali quickly read the mood in the house and switched the conversation. Well, it's their life I suppose. Don't get me wrong I pray for the best for them. Mahmoud's phone started vibrating. He could see a foreign number and knew it was Fareed.

"Hello Fareed. How are you. We have just been talking about you with Uncle Ali. Yes, he is here. He arrived yesterday. He had a good trip although a bit anxious. Say hello to him." There was a grin on Ali's face as he pressed the phone to his ear.

"Hallo Fareed. I thought I would find you here. I didn't know that you had a job in New York. You are very fortunate young man. Hey, who is this girl I hear about? Your mum and dad just told me you are serious. Fareed quickly summarised his relationship.

"Uncle, you will love her when you meet. She is Godsend. I did not know that God still made them so beautiful in Zimbabwe." They both laughed, and you could tell that whatever uncle Ali thought before, he had been neutralised.

"Oh, don't make me laugh. You are always funny Fareed. Yes, I look forward to meeting her one day. But be careful.

Don't rush. Take your time. Give me what? Uncle Ali seemed surprised. You want her to phone me".

"Yes uncle. She is working in Los Angeles. She will call you and then you can interrogate her, ha-ha. Don't have a heart attack uncle. One day you will come to the wedding." Fareed gave his final word. These two had so much in common. When Fareed was growing up, Uncle Ali became very close to him. Although he was no longer Muslim, he maintained a close relationship hoping that one day his uncle would have a relationship with Jesus.

"Oh, thank you Fareed." uncle retorted It was a relief for Fareed. He thanked God for the way this conversation had gone. He called Susan straightaway to deliver the good news.

No one could have imagined the way this relationship had gone. Months of prayer and steadfastness were paying off. They began to believe that they were meant for each other. Cross cultural relationships were indeed a challenge but, with God's help, it could be done. They were witnessing changes in attitude from both families. They prayed that this would continue until their wedding one day and beyond. Susan could not wait to stand tall as best maid at Melissa's wedding. They would learn a thing or two before theirs. And as for Keith and Fareed both girls knew that they would also become real friends. Diverse families made from heaven.

Susan continued to ward off brothers from her local church who believed that the best marriages were black on black. She sometimes became frustrated by the new doctrine of same colour marriages which she knew were not biblical but had become the new currency. And because Fareed was thousands of miles away, she sometimes became vulnerable, but she soldiered on. So, every day she had to call Fareed and share her frustrations.

"Fareed, you know this Desmond I met after church in the church car park. He has become a pain. He lectures me on the doom and gloom of cross-cultural marriages and the disasters he has witnessed in the USA. He does not say anything good. His mum is anti-white. When he fell in love with a Korean girl, his mum would not even shake hands with her and yet she is active in church." "Susan, Susan, this is the reality everywhere. I am under the same pressure here. But what is important is what God says about it. You remember Miriam, Moses' sister, she was punished by God when she accused her brother of marrying a foreigner. You must read that chapter. I am sure it will not be easy, but it is doable I can assure you. If uncle Ali is now on our side, it means miracles still happen." They both laughed. They were ready for the storms because of whom they believed in.

"Ok Susan, I will hear from you about Melissa and Keith's preparation. We must see them both before it happens."

"It's ok I will mention this to Melissa. We can either fly to the UK or they can come to New York. The two of us can book into a hotel and you boys can put up at your apartment "Sue you are a genius. Bye"

Melissa and Keith had become so busy at work and at church. There was a demand for them to speak to small groups of young men and women who were desperate to get as much help as they could concerning their future. And as solicitors and committed Christians who so far had overcome some of the hostility towards their budding relationship, they were the right people in town to help. Sometimes they spoke together to mixed groups, and other times it was one to one counselling. On one occasion they were in conversation with parents who needed help to cope with the decisions their children were about to take. They became the living example of how it was possible for diverse cultures to intermingle. They sincerely believed that for them it was a combination of their love for each other and the reconciling effect of the Jesus they had embraced. Theirs was not merely a religious commitment but a relational commitment. They talked to Jesus, walked with him, and could hang out with him in different environments. Theirs was a relationship. And this resonated well with the many youngsters who were searching for the truth and someone to hold on to. They saw people as images of the creator who made them and not as compartmentalised tribal groupings. Love became the common denominator in forging new relationships and revamping the struggling ones. Their world had become transformed, and they were reminded of the words from the Bible, 'If anyone says I love God, but hates his brother, he is a liar; for he who does not love his brother whom he has seen cannot love God whom he has not seen' 1 John 4:20 ESV. Loving God means loving everybody. This was Jesus's mantra. Loving your enemy was a characteristic of a true follower of Christ. Melissa and Keith in a way were trying to live like Jesus even though sometimes they struggled. And every time they met young men and women struggling, they communicated that message and showcased their relationship as evidence that it was possible, with God's help.

Chapter 27
The future revealed

Since talking to Susan about meeting somewhere before their wedding, Melissa and Keith had to decide on a possible dates.

"Keith, it has to be in the next three weeks, otherwise we won't find the time to arrange to see Susan and Fareed before our wedding", Melissa put the speaker on loud as she prepared a ham sandwich in the kitchen.

"What's that rattling noise", Keith asked as if he hadn't worked out that he had been put on hold. "Making a sandwich dear, cutting down on costs, eh, "Melissa giggled.

"Friday, the 5th until Sunday the seventh. I can make it there if we can get a flight that leaves around 7 pm. I would have to drive to Heathrow and leave the car there or we can meet up and go together.", Keith was already online searching for the tickets as he spoke.

"Keith that's ok. I can take my leave day on Friday, so I don't have to rush. That's fine with me. Check for the tickets. Norwegian is normally cheap if we take a direct flight to New York." Susan confirmed.

That was it. They would fly together to New York and planned that the two girls would stay in one of the Marriot

Hotels near the airport. They could not believe that this was happening. Keith from Oxford, Fareed from Iraq, now Qatar and the two beauties from Zimbabwe.

There was no way to put it. This was indeed a unity in diversity. A consequence of decisions that took them to the Diaspora. A demonstration of how in the eyes of the Creator, we are all one cut from the same cloth. Their visit to New York would take them to Fareed's church in New York which was very diverse.

How time flies, Fareed thought as he sat in the Metro coach on his way to JFK airport. Susan would arrive first from LA and then Melissa and Keith on the Norwegian airline from Heathrow. Fareed had mixed feelings. He had not made either Melissa or Keith before except for what he had been told by Susan. Most of it biased, of course. That morning he had read from the book of Acts chapter eleven, where Peter was asked to speak to the Gentiles. And suddenly, the Holy Spirit whom Peter thought was the preserve of the chosen nation the Jews was poured to these foreigners. God seemed to have a sense of humour. He always did the impossible and the unexpected. He always proves others wrong. He indeed is the protocol breaker! Where there is hatred he brings love, where there is disunity, he blends people together. He sees the bigger picture. And here he was, *Fareed thought, an Arab but a believer in Christ meeting up with Keith, British, who too loved the Lord Jesus. Life has strange ways,* he thought. Susan's plane had just landed as Fareed stood at the exit lounge for passengers. He waved as he saw the elegant figure of his loving friend. She ran toward him pulling a small case and a tiny handbag. They hugged furiously as a compensation for not kissing. As usual Susan started crying as she was led along. They hopped in the metro, which had just stopped and were on their way to the Marriot just for Susan to freshen up before they went back to receive Melissa and Keith.

An hour later Susan and Fareed were back at the airport to receive Keith and Melissa. In the arrival concourse, there was pandemonium as Susan and Fareed received their guests. There was screaming, hugging, laughing as they all staggered through the lounge. The boys could only watch. Keith, typical British introduced himself as Fareed did the Middle Eastern greeting, this time with the customary hugs and kisses to the chick. Fortunately, Keith was aware and expected it.

"Look at them. It seems we are not wanted here". Keith broke the ice as they followed behind.

"Sorry guys we were speaking in Shona. I am sure you expected it," Melissa retreated to join the boys.

"We thought you were speaking in tongues", Fareed laughingly retorted. The language of the heart had now taken over and the boys were prepared for it, but they had never quite seen it in action. "Oh, Keith this is Susan, Fareed, this is me, Melissa.", Melissa burst into laughter. It felt like they were at the united nations with languages ready to explode in unison under a multi-coloured rainbow.

For some reason they talked and talked like they had been together before. And as they continued, Fareed interrupted and asked that they just thank God for his goodness. They all burst into song and from then on it was just worship and singing punctuated by prayers of thanksgiving. They all realised how good God had been to them and here they were a few months before Melissa and Keith's wedding. Susan kept looking at Melissa and Keith, her cheeks drenched in tears. Melissa joined her and what a sight! Their relationships meant a lot to them and because of what they had experienced, they were forever grateful. They knew the battle still loomed large on the horizon, but thus far the Lord had been good to them. They shared their stories and the striving to stay together. They reflected on their parents' attitudes and how somehow, they were able to navigate this route effectively by getting most of the relatives on board.

They had dinner at Fareed's; it was a takeaway pizza. They did not want to go out. That was reserved for Saturday night after the movie. The girls took an Uber taxi back to Marriot hotel and it was past midnight when they started to doze off. Susan shared her soul and so did Melissa. Then prayers again and songs and more songs. It was like a nightmare happening.

"Melissa, I can't believe you will be Mrs Keith asikana. Mwari wakanaka (Girl, God is good) "Hey, veku Middle East (you from the Middle East) Melissa teased Susan. She knew that Susan had taken on a bigger challenge but when she saw Fareed at the airport, she saw a gracious man whose life had been bowled over by Jesus Christ. That was what mattered most.

Fareed took a bit of persuading when at dinner Keith and Melissa asked him to be one of the men of honour. This came as a surprise as Fareed thought that he really was the new kid on the block, and it would be unfair not to give the chance to some of Keith's close friends. Melissa and Keith would not have it and

Fareed lost. His next challenge was deciding on a suit to wear. Susan was already on the list as maid of honour." I hope you guys will be able to arrive in the UK a few days before, "Keith began to do what he was good at. Planning! By the time they went their separate ways for the night, they were all tired and looked forward to the Sunday service at Fareed's new church.

There was an hour between their departures and as Melissa and Keith disappeared behind the Immigration area, Susan and Fareed had a moment to say their intimate goodbyes. She too disappeared and Fareed took the lift down to the Metro station. What a weekend he thought as he started checking messages on his phone for the first time.

The next chapter in their lives would be more interesting they thought. Children, in laws, and the lot. All because they had relocated to foreign lands which had now become home. Questions for Fareed and Susan still lingered. Would they be married in the USA, Zimbabwe, or Qatar? Where would they live permanently after they tied the knot? How would they forever be able to navigate the storms of prejudice, racism, and downright bigotry? They always thought about Jesus; how he set the example. In his struggle with those who were racist, prejudiced, and evil, he remained resolute and demonstrated a love that no one could match. Such love diffused the ambers of hatred and bigotry. It neutralised the enemy and made him stand out as a beacon of light in a sea of darkness. That was the template they were going to use if they were to survive in this jungle that was riddled with sin and shame. And it would work if they stuck to the Jesus script. Many applauded them and they too became role models to many young men and women who were keen to join the multicultural love bandwagon. Their story became a real story, written and unwritten which began to spread wherever they went. They bulldozed the feelings of hate and built bridges wherever they went. They sometimes stumbled and fell but quickly picked themselves up and kept following the Jesus they adored. Soon there was no Arab, English, or African but couples whose bonds were bound by cords that could not be broken. For now, it was all systems go as plans for their weddings now gained momentum. Only God could have worked this out!

Ingram Content Group UK Ltd.
Milton Keynes UK
UKHW012014100423
419951UK00014B/247/J